Eucharist and Ecumenism

Dedicated to Elaine Park

Contents

Foreword

IN THIS "LITTLE BOOK" of essays, as he describes it, Owen F. Cummings groups fourteen illuminating liturgical works and/or personalities by eucharistic theme and ecumenical genre, placing them in the broader context of their own worlds. Employing an exceptionally lucid and accessible writing style worthy of his Scottish heritage, he reveals a unique contribution of each one as he invites his readers to share his own love of the liturgy and his commitment to Christian unity. With the eminent Geoffrey Wainwright, liturgical theologian and ecumenist, as model, Cummings takes his readers on a journey of discovery into the merging world of ecumenism and worship with as guide "history, the real theology of liberation."

While a perfect companion to his recent works of related content like *Canterbury Cousins: The Eucharist in Contemporary Anglican Theology* (2007) and *Eucharistic Doctors* (2005), this one "is not your father's Oldsmobile," so to speak, as it fills in surprising *lacunae*, covering significant yet often little known "liturgical personalities." Beginning with expected formative works such as the *Didache*, Justin, and Hippolytus the reader is invited to a greater appreciation also of Sarapion as well as Addai and Mari through remarkable Medievals like Margery Kempe, courageous Caroline Divines, Revivalists on the American Frontier, key contributors to liturgical renewal before and after Vatican Council II, and finally of the unsuspected Graham Greene's *Monsignor Quixote*.

Owen F. Cummings, with his extensive education in the United Kingdom and Ireland, his years of service as Roman Catholic Deacon, and with his experience as educator in the United States and abroad, demonstrates his mastery of historical theology through the lenses of the liturgy and ecumenism. Conversant in a special way with nineteenth- and twentieth-century-historians, biographers, commentators, and fellow theologians of history—the quality that guarantees the substance of these essays—Cummings is above all a keen interpreter of historical persons, a master storyteller, and, as readers will discover for themselves, a "biographer's biographer." The diversity of persons and works treated here reflects the reality of the marriage of life and liturgy across time and worship traditions. Essay after essay argues persuasively how much alike Western Christians at worship really are, without ever falling into the easy trap of superficial relativity.

To this point, Cummings writes in conclusion to one of his chapters, "The cause of Christian unity cannot be well served until theologians and liturgists study carefully the 'great cloud of witnesses' who have gone ahead of us. Without careful study of the past and of one another's past we shall remain fixed in our own theological and liturgical insularity." This commitment is what makes this "little book" of essays such a valuable contribution to both the academy and to a broad readership beyond the classroom. Unpretentious, soundly liturgical, and ecumenically prophetic, it accomplishes its straightforward goal most effectively. Cummings successfully creates his hoped for ambience wherein "talking about God needs to yield to talking to God." Indeed, he allows each author or work that speaks in the book to do just that, and this is what one remembers most about each one.

The Rev. Richard Rutherford
Professor of Theology,
University of Portland

Preface

PHILOSOPHER OF RELIGION TURNED popular psychologist, Sam Keen, somewhere relates that when he went to Harvard Divinity School as a student, one of the faculty remarked that "We study religion here, we don't much practice it." Of course, it is necessary to study religion with all the tools of modern scholarship. There comes a point, however, when talking about God needs to yield to talking *to* God. Not everyone, perhaps, experiences this. Both the context and the circumstances of one's life can get in the way, preventing the conjunction of talking about and talking to God. For a believing Christian, talking to God, that is to say relationship with God, is not merely a point of in-depth study, but rather a moral and existential necessity. It is so beautifully illustrated by Psalm 23. In that poem the psalmist moves from third-person language of God to second-person language. He moves from talking *about* God—"The Lord is my shepherd," etc.—to those two (at least in Hebrew!) magnificent words: "You with-me." That is the hoped for ambience of this book.

Unfortunately, Christians from the various denominations do not worship together very much. We remain very much within the enclaves (or is it comfort zones?) of our own particular traditions. It may be the case that, as William Temple put it last century, the ecumenical movement is the great new fact of our time, but the project of Christian unity tends to stay on the periphery of most peoples' Christian vision. Yet, it has to be said that in the last forty years or so liturgical theology and ecumenism have often gone hand in hand. The all too slow reaching out of Christians to one another, in search of deeper degrees of communion in order to affect a more persuasive witness of the gospel to the world, has also brought them to a much deeper awareness of the centrality of liturgy/worship, and especially of the Eucharist. One of the classic exemplars of this fruitful coincidence of liturgy and ecumenism in our time is the Methodist theologian, Geoffrey

Wainwright (born in 1939), now retired from Duke Divinity School. Wainwright is a passionate ecumenist, and has been all his life. Wainwright is equally passionate about liturgy. It was the focus of his doctoral dissertation on the Eucharist and eschatology at Geneva, and he has written an outstanding one-volume systematic theology with the apt title, *Doxology: The Praise of God in Worship, Doctrine and Life*. Wainwright has consistently brought ecumenism and liturgy into a mutually fruitful co-inherence, as witnessed by his wide-ranging bibliography. This book seeks to follow in its own fashion the way of Wainwright. It seeks to bring into life-giving interplay liturgy and Christian unity.

The book seeks to do this in various ways. It moves historically, in the conviction that church history is the real theology of liberation, liberating Christians from so many of their ill-founded presuppositions, especially about one another. It scrolls very selectively through the traditions of Christian worship, attempting to achieve two goals. First, to draw attention to some of the earliest descriptions of liturgy and liturgical practice in a way that is accessible to the average theological reader. This is especially the case in chapters 1–5, focusing on key patristic liturgical texts and authors. In these chapters the hope is not simply to provide knowledge about our worshiping Christian forebears, but also to inspire present-day Christians to learn from their example. Theological writing today is witnessing a renaissance of interest in the theological texts of the first six centuries. Chapters 1–5 explore some of the liturgical, and especially eucharistic texts of these centuries. While my hope is to use solid historical scholarship in the exegesis of these texts, I want to do more. I want to help Christians of today see something of the beauty of these texts, and find inspiration from them for their own Christian living and worshiping. The earliest Christians are followed in chapters 6 and 7 by having regard to some medieval Christians—a medieval Archbishop of Canterbury, Baldwin of Ford along with some of his friends and peers, and then the late medieval English laywoman, Margery Kempe. If the former represents theological and ecclesiastical leadership, the latter shows us a profound appreciation of liturgy and life at the ordinary level of the laity, even if Margery Kempe cannot be counted as merely "ordinary." Chapters 8, 9, and 10 move on to consider three key Anglican contributors to liturgy and liturgical theology: Richard Hooker, Lancelot Andrewes, and John Keble. Each of them represents in his time some of the best of the Anglican tradition of worship, and so each of them constitutes a gift to the wider Christian worshiping community. The Anglican contribution is continued in chapter 12 with an appreciation of the liturgist Ronald Jasper, and to a lesser extent his son David Jasper, Professor of Theology and Literature at the University of Glasgow, Scotland. Chapter 13 looks at a Catholic contemporary of the elder Jasper, James Dunlop Crichton, whose many books and publications mediated to the generation immediately consequent upon Vatican II an understanding of the revised Roman rites and a fresh appreciation of liturgy as such. Chapter 11 moves away from these Anglican-Catholic traditions to consider, admittedly in all too brief a fashion, the liturgical and eucharistic contribution of "frontier revivalism" through the remarkable book of liturgist Kimberly Long on this subject. Long points out, in often surprising ways, how a revivalist Protestant tradition in America also draws upon deep liturgical and eucharistic wells. Finally, chapter 14 turns to the twentieth-century novelist Graham Greene's *Monsignor Quixote*. This may seem strange in a book that explores Christian worship from an ecumenical point of view. Towards the end of this novel the fictional Monsignor Quixote celebrates a fictional Eucharist, but the questions raised by Greene in this section of his novel are key to a genuine understanding of liturgy and life. Maybe the broader perspective opened up by Greene could be considered a wider liturgical ecumenism.

It is the author's hope that this little book will make a modest contribution to the love of liturgy and of Christian unity. Christians must become aware of one another's liturgical traditions. When we begin to do so, we will find that some of our presuppositions about Christian sisters and brothers may not be entirely accurate. We may even find that we are much closer than we initially thought. At least, that is the author's hope and prayer.

1

The Didache and the Eucharist

The "Eucharistic" prayers in chapters 9 f . . . are quite unparalleled. Their strong eschatological flavor and phraseology and the description of Christ as "Thy Servant Jesus" strike a very primitive note.

FRANK L. CROSS[1]

IN THE HALCYON DAYS of the early 1970s I was a graduate student reading for the BD in the Anglican School of Divinity of Trinity College Dublin, in fact the first Roman Catholic to graduate with this degree since the foundation of the college by Queen Elizabeth I in 1592. My thesis supervisor was the Rev. Prof. Frederick Ercolo Vokes (1910–2000), Archbishop King Professor of Divinity. Prof. Vokes had published in 1938 *The Riddle of the Didache,* and this book was my first serious encounter with this early Christian liturgical text.[2] It has remained an interest ever since. Still in the early stages of *Didache* research, Prof. Vokes from our vantage point today got some things wrong, most notably his dating of the document. He provides a very late dating of the text—"in the last third of the second century or first third of the third century."[3] A growing number of scholars, constituting perhaps a consensus, put the origin of *The Didache* much earlier, before or towards the end of the first century. Nonetheless, with careful attention to philological detail and patristic research at the time, *The Riddle of the Didache* still repays close reading. The amount of research that has been conducted in the last twenty-five or thirty years on *The Didache* is overwhelming and indeed sometimes encyclopedic, especially the work of

Kurt Niederwimmer and Aaron Milavec.⁴ My more recent interest in the text has come about through reading the eminently clear and always lively book by the Irish historical and liturgical theologian Thomas O'Loughlin, *The Didache: A Window on the Earliest Christians.*⁵

Introducing *The Didache*

The text of *The Didache*, in a codex probably to be dated to 1056, was discovered and published by the Metropolitan of Nicomedia, Philotheos Bryennios, in 1883, and that publication has been described as follows: "The discovery of *The Didache* caused in Victorian Europe and America something of the stir aroused by the discovery of the Dead Sea Scrolls in the Judaean Desert in the years following the Second World War."⁶ There may be an element of hyperbole in that description, but it remains beyond doubt that this text has complemented much of what had been known of early Christian worship. As noted above, *The Didache* is dated in a variety of ways by the scholarly community, but a date in the last quarter of the first century seems to have gained a consensus. This makes the text contemporary with the canonical Gospels. The author is unknown.⁷

The Didache falls into two parts. Part One, chapters 1–6, is taken up with the "Two Ways"—as in Psalm 1, the Way of Life and the Way of Death—and is concerned with moral teaching and conduct. Part Two, chapters 7–16, focuses for the most part on Christian worship, and provides a description of the Eucharist celebrated on the Lord's Day. While the great eucharistic theologian and patristic scholar Johannes Betz is accurate in stating that "the famous meal prayers of chapters 9 and 10 are among the most difficult and contested problems of *Didache* research"—perhaps especially in terms of their origins and in relation to pre-existent euchological forms—the consensus of theological as well as exegetical scholarship today seems content basically to recognize the meal prayers as arising out of the Eucharist.⁸ It is true that there are problems and particularly the fact that the text begins with the cup, not the bread, which is to say the least very unusual in a eucharistic context. Betz goes on to say that "the sayings in these verses [chapters 9–10] offer a pronounced eucharistic color which can hardly be ignored."⁹ Betz solves the problem by proposing that the prayers of *Didache* 9–10 "were transformed and revalued from original eucharistic prayers to mere agape prayers," the agape meal being an actual meal celebrated in common by the earliest Christians.¹⁰ Scientifically and methodologically Betz may be on the right track. Scholarly and scientific concerns are not locked in opposition to pastoral-liturgical concerns. That would be an impossible situation. But perhaps there is more to be said. While this is not the appropriate place to develop the methodological argument, one might propose that alongside the empirical data of text and ritual there is also what might be called an informal *sensus communis fidelium*/common sense of the faithful, a constant and continuous tradition of eucharistic worship that provides a "nose" for what empirical liturgical data may not yield. That is the position taken here, that is to say, that in *Didache* 9–10 we have an agape/community meal in which the Eucharist is celebrated. Still, a real meal was going on after which in all likelihood occurred the celebration of the Eucharist. In point of fact, if this is actually the case, it coheres well with the meal practice of Jesus: "The disciples become the assembly around the table and there bless the Father in the way that they believed Jesus did."[11] Let us acquaint ourselves with this assembly of the *Didache* around the table for the actual Eucharist.

The Text[12]

9. Concerning the Eucharist, eucharistize in this way. Begin with the chalice: "We give thanks to thee, our Father, for the holy Vine of thy servant David, which thou hast made known to us through thy Servant Jesus."

"Glory be to thee, world without end."

Then over the broken bread: "We give thanks to thee, our Father, for the life and knowledge thou has made known to us through thy Servant Jesus."

"Glory be to thee, world without end."

"As this broken bread, once dispersed over the hills, was brought together and became one loaf, so may thy church be brought together from the ends of the earth into thy kingdom."

"Thine is the glory and the power, through Jesus Christ, forever and ever."

No one is to eat or drink of your Eucharist but those who have been baptized in the name of the Lord; for the Lord's own saying applies here, "Give not that which is holy unto dogs."

10. When all have partaken sufficiently, give thanks in these words: "Thanks be to thee, holy Father, for thy sacred name which thou hast

caused to dwell in our hearts, and for the knowledge and faith and immortality which thou hast revealed to us through thy servant Jesus."

"Glory be to thee for ever and ever."

"Thou, O Almighty Lord, hast created all things for thine own name's sake; to all men thou hast given meat and drink to enjoy, that they may give thanks to thee, but to us thou hast graciously given spiritual meat and drink, together with life eternal, through thy Servant. Especially, and above all, do we give thanks to thee for the mightiness of thy power."

"Glory be to thee for ever and ever."

"Be mindful of thy church, O Lord; deliver it from all evil, perfect it in thy love, sanctify it, and gather it from the four winds into the kingdom which thou hast prepared for it."

"Thine is the power and the glory forever and ever."

"Let Grace come, and this present world pass away."

"Hosanna to the God of David."

"Whosoever is holy, let him approach. Whoso is not, let him repent."

"Maranatha. Amen."

(Prophets, however, should be free to give thanks as they please.)

14. Assemble on the Lord's Day, and break bread and offer the Eucharist; but first make confession of your faults, so that your sacrifice may be a pure one. Anyone who has a difference with his fellow is not to take part with you until they have been reconciled, so as to avoid any profanation of your sacrifice. For this is the offering of which the Lord has said, "Everywhere and always bring me a sacrifice that is undefiled, for I am a great King, says the Lord, and my name is the wonder of nations."

Commentary

What liturgical theologian Arthur Couratin said of the texts of the New Testament applies equally to such texts as *The Didache*: "The books of the New Testament do not provide us with a handbook to the life of the church of the first century. For the most part they are occasional writings, each produced to meet some particular set of circumstances."[13] In other words, we ought not to look to these ancient texts for what they simply cannot provide. The text immediately has its own challenges. It does not contain, for example, the words of institution that we find in the Synoptic Gospels' accounts of the Last Supper, as well as in the celebration of the Eucharist today—"This is my body. . . . This is my blood." That particular challenge is really a false one. "The notion that the Eucharist burst onto the scene at the Last Supper with the formal priesthood, specific words and a fixed theology does not allow for the fact that all religious structures change over time, evolving with some aspects becoming clearer and others more obscure."[14] That is to read into *The Didache* the concerns of much later Christian generations. What we find through careful attention to the text is that the Eucharist was celebrated in the context of a community meal, much like the situation of St. Paul's Corinth in 1 Corinthians 11. The cup and the bread are blessed, and when the meal is complete, there are prayers of thanksgiving. There are repeated doxologies, in all likelihood congregational responses, and, as in the Staniforth-Louth edition these doxologies are rendered in italics.

The Jewish dimension of the prayers is very clear. Some examples: "the holy Vine of thy servant David" as a description of the church; the various references to the name of God; the emphasis on the coming kingdom of God. The very first words in chapter 9 are *peri tes eucharistias,* "concerning the Eucharist." This word *eucharistia* literally means "thanksgiving," and is not necessarily and immediately a reference to the Eucharist as such. However, the context that unfolds with the chapter seems persuasively to suggest that it means here the celebration of the Eucharist. Ronald Jasper, the Anglican liturgist about whom we shall read in chapter 12, and his colleague Geoffrey Cuming maintain that "the liturgical sense is possible," and that "the rubric at the end of chapter 9 seems more appropriate to a Eucharist."[15] The Eucharist begins interestingly with the chalice in chapter 9. A Trinitarian, or at the very least a binitarian note is struck as thanks are given to the Father for the holy Vine that is the church and by apparent implication the eucharistic wine through his Servant Jesus. This is a wonderful example of eucharistic ecclesiology, with the eucharistic wine making the Vine of the church. Jesus is described as "servant." The Greek word is *pais,* a word that can mean "child" or "servant." It is possible that the word is polyvalent, including both meanings. Jesus is "child/son of God" and, intentionally in some texts, the "(suffering) servant of God."[16] Then the doxology occurs, "Glory be to thee, world without end." Again, thanks are given to the Father over the broken bread through his Servant Jesus, and the doxology is repeated.

The unity of the church throughout the world is given emphasis, a unity that is both present and yet to come in its fullness in the future: "As this broken bread, once dispersed over the hills, was brought together and became one loaf, so may thy Church be brought together from the ends of the earth into thy kingdom." The "broken bread, once dispersed over the hills" may reflect the text of John 6:12: "Gather up the fragments left over, that nothing may be lost," and "became one loaf" may reflect 1 Corinthians 10:17: "Because there is one bread, we who are many are one body, for we all partake of the one bread." At the very least we are entitled to conclude about these scriptural echoes if not quotations, that the traditions that have come to exist as the New Testament were already in wide circulation in the first century. Now the doxology, though intentionally the same, changes verbally, "Thine is the glory and the power through Jesus Christ, forever and ever."

There follows an admonition to the effect that the Eucharist is to be received only by the baptized. The quotation, "Give not that which is holy unto dogs," is taken from Matthew 7:6, indicating perhaps that not only is the Gospel of St. Matthew in circulation by this time, but also that Matthew and *The Didache* may both come from the Christian community in Antioch, the most important Christian center in the first century.[17]

Chapter 10 speaks of the agape/the community meal, "When all have partaken sufficiently." It moves on to a prayer of thanksgiving for the gift of Servant Jesus, and, once more, there is a doxology. Thanks should be given to God by all people for their food and drink, and special thanks should be given by Christians for the "spiritual meat and drink" of the Eucharist, through Servant Jesus. Again, there is a doxology.

A prayer is now made for the church, for its protection, its perfection in love, its sanctification, and its eschatological unity "from the four winds into the kingdom." The last part of chapter 10 comes to beautiful expression in the prayer for Christ's final coming, "Let Grace come." "Grace" can only mean here Jesus Christ.[18] Another doxology is given, reminiscent of the *Sanctus,* "Hosanna to the God of David." This is followed by an encouragement to repentance and holiness, and once more by a prayer for Christ's final coming, "Maranatha. Amen." *Maranatha* is an Aramaic word, reflecting undoubtedly the prayer practice of the very earliest Christians, and it is capable of being translated in two ways: "The Lord has come" and "Our Lord, come!" May we see in the understanding of the Eucharist here both the Incarnation—"The Lord has come"—and the Parousia—"Our Lord, come!" This is the point of view adumbrated by Methodist liturgical theologian, Geoffrey Wainwright, when he says: "The *Maranatha* is to be understood in a double sense: it is a prayer for the parousia ('Come, Lord!'), and a confession of the Lord's sacramental advent in the Eucharist ('The Lord has come!')."[19] This enables the Eucharist to function "as the bridge between the first and the second Parousia."[20]

The most obvious liturgical genre for the entirety of chapter 10 is an incipient eucharistic prayer, although it must be admitted strictly that "it does not seem possible to reach an unassailable conclusion on the available evidence."[21] The available evidence may not yield a full-blown eucharistic prayer, but it may provide us with "hints."[22] Thus, Hans Lietzmann has argued very persuasively that we may find in this chapter 10 a kind of liturgical dialogue between the one who presides and the congregation, the kind of liturgical dialogue that is intrinsic to the eucharistic prayer:[23]

> Presider: "Let Grace come, and this present world pass away."
> Congregation: "Hosanna to the son of David."
> Presider: "Whosoever is holy, let him approach. Whoso is not, let him repent. Maranatha."
> Congregation: "Amen."

Perhaps we may speculate that this liturgical dialogue follows the ending of the agape/community meal and marks the beginning of the eucharistic liturgy proper, a liturgy which the text does not actually go on to describe. Again speculatively, it may even be the case that the "*Maranatha*/Come, Lord!" was spoken by the congregation at the inception of the eucharistic liturgy, in Geoffrey Wainwright's words, "[when the Lord] is at this very moment making his entry into the midst of the congregation."[24]

Chapter 14 reminds us that the earliest name for Sunday was the "Lord's Day," reflecting the Easter day of Resurrection, the day marked centrally by the celebration of the Eucharist. That Eucharist may not be celebrated without acknowledging one's sins and repentance, and most especially without reconciliation in the eucharistic community, reflecting the words of the Lord in the Sermon on the Mount in Matthew 5:23–24: "First be reconciled to your brother, and then offer your gift." Finally, in chapter 14 we find this note on the Eucharist as sacrifice. "For this is the offering of which the Lord has said, 'Everywhere and always bring me a sacrifice that is undefiled, for I am a great king, says the Lord, and my name is the wonder of nations.'" The quotation comes from the prophet Malachi and was popular among the early Christians, being used, for example, by Justin, Irenaeus, and Tertullian.

Who Presided at the Eucharist?

The earliest eucharistic communities of which the eucharistic community of *The Didache* was one met, of course, in one another's homes. These were house churches. That raises the interesting question of who presided at the Eucharist, a question that has become somewhat neuralgic in our times. The immediate answer is: "We simply do not know for sure!" It would be sheerly anachronistic to read the later protocols of ordination back into these earliest texts. We do not know enough about eucharistic leadership in the first century to provide an absolutely accurate answer.[25] At the end of chapter 10 we read: "Prophets, however, should be free to give thanks as they please." In other words, "prophets," probably to be understood as charismatic leaders/teachers, may freely improvise at the Eucharist as best they know how.

What about other presiders? Thomas O'Loughlin, in his recent book on *The Didache,* provides a fine paragraph that is very helpful in this regard. Let us quote it at length and then make some comments:

> We can imagine a situation like this in those early decades. At the Sunday gathering whoever was considered one of the leaders of the community—and remember this took place in a house so it would not have been a large gathering—took the lead in making the thanksgiving at the meal. But at other times, whoever was the head of the table—the householder—took the lead. So when one Christian hosted a meal for other Christians, that person took the lead. The assumption of *The Didache* is that every Christian should know these prayers for celebrating a eucharistic meal—perhaps the ideal it aspired to was that no meal would be shared without the Father being thanked for his gifts and his gift of Jesus—and so we can assume that every Christian was expected to have use of this skill from time to time. Indeed, if the "prophets"—who seem to have been the experts in the Way—are allowed to use whatever form of prayer they wish, then the fact that these prayers are laid out in full presumes that everyone else needed a learned formula; this in turn presumes that every Christian may have use for such a formula.[26]

It needs to be acknowledged from the outset that O'Loughlin has no particular ministerial axe to grind. Throughout his book he wishes to describe as accurately but as simply as possible *The Didache* as a window on the earliest Christians. And so what do we notice in this passage? First, that the Christian gathering would have been relatively small because it fitted into someone's house. Second, one of the designated Christian leaders would have taken the initiative in presiding at the community meal/Eucharist. Third, on other such occasions the householder would have taken this role. Fourth, all adult Christians would have been expected, at least in principle, to know what to do in this context, and so would have needed what we might call "a basic eucharistic formula" that they could use when called upon. Needless to say, the liturgical and ecclesiological provision later in the tradition is rather different. However, if we are trying to be fair to the paucity of evidence that we actually have, it will be recognized with the early church historian William H. C. Frend that doctrinal "musts" rarely match historical "facts" with the exactitude that later generations may have come to expect.[27]

Conclusion

The patristic scholar, Willy Rordorf ends a very fine essay on *The Didache* with two practical and pastoral conclusions. First of all, recognizing that the community of *The Didache* would have been a small community that celebrated both its community meal and the Eucharist, he asks, "Could we not have both forms of the Eucharist in our churches?" Rordorf means that contemporary Christian communities need both human intimacy, the intimacy that is expressive of real communion and is expressed in dining together, as well as the intimacy of the divine communion that comes to expression in the celebration of the Eucharist. Both in his judgment are needed. Who would quarrel with that today? Secondly, Rordorf belongs to a Reformation tradition, and so he is cognizant of the sad fact that Christians are so separated from the table of the Lord even in our avowedly ecumenical age. Since each community recognizes with the author of our text that it is but a small fragment of the universal Body of Christ, there should be fervent prayer and effective action for the visible unity of all Christians.[28] We could do worse than to take Willy Rordorf's conclusions to heart, and we could do worse than to read Thomas O'Loughlin's very satisfying book on *The Didache*.

2

Justin and the Eucharist

Justin has left us many short works, the products of a cultured mind deeply versed in theology. They are full of good things, and I can recommend them to students, indicating those that have come usefully to my knowledge.

EUSEBIUS, *HISTORY OF THE CHURCH*, 4.18

The most important second-century apologist was Justin "the Martyr."

ROBERT M. GRANT[29]

Justin was one of the most original thinkers Christianity produced.

ERIC F. OSBORN[30]

Who Was Justin?

THE ACCOLADES THAT INTRODUCE this chapter on "Justin and the Eucharist" from the earliest church historian, Eusebius, and from two contemporary patristic scholars, Robert Grant and Eric Osborn, give us an initial sense of his importance and achievement. In histories of Christian doctrine Justin is usually classified as one of the "Apologists." The Apologists were Christian writers of the second century who composed various addresses and pleas to Roman Emperors and others in public authority on behalf of their fellow Christians. It needs to be recalled that Christianity was not judged a legal religion, and therefore to be tolerated, before the Edict of Milan and the Emperor Constantine (311/312). Global persecution of the Christian faith was relatively rare, but spontaneous local persecutions were rather frequent, often based on envy and greed. The Apologists were intent on showing that Christianity was no subversive political phenomenon. "The aim of [their] writings was in general to persuade the authorities that the frequent local persecutions of Christians were unjust, unnecessary, and unworthy of enlightened rulers."[31] Justin, perhaps more often referred to as Justin Martyr, is the best known of these Apologists.

He was born in the late first or early second century, "Justin, son of Priscus and grandson of Baccius, of Flavia Neapolis in Syrian Palestine."[32] His birthplace has frequently been in the news due to the Palestinian-Israeli conflict, and is known today as the city of Nablus in the West Bank. Justin is one of those interesting individuals who seems to have found his way into the Christian community primarily through an intense intellectual journey.[33] He drifted to the Western Asia Minor city of Ephesus "where, like many other young men, he went the rounds of the philosophical teachers."[34] He found himself singularly dissatisfied with the various schools—Stoics, Peripatetics, Pythagoreans, Platonists. Summarizing Justin, he found that the Stoic was unable or unwilling to discuss theological matters; the Peripatetic was too subtle and too fond of money, and demanded excessive tuition fees; the Pythagorean demanded pre-registration credits that Justin did not have—music, astronomy, geometry. Finally, he discovered a Platonist and fell in love with Platonic philosophy, and one can see why. There is an architectonic beauty to the Platonic vision of reality, and it was to sustain Justin, but not forever.

Near the sea one day as he was meditating, he met an unnamed old man who cross-examined him on the problems of Platonic thought, and through this old man he was led to Christianity. He describes his experience: "Immediately, a fire sprang up in my soul. I was possessed by a longing for the prophets and for those men who are friends of Christ. And as I turned over his words in my mind, I discovered that this philosophy alone is trustworthy and profitable. It is in this sense and for this reason that I am a philosopher," words written in his Dialogue with Trypho, about 130 AD.[35]

Justin then traveled to Rome, the capital of the Roman Empire, and opened a school in his house, probably an apartment since it is described as being "above Myrtinus's baths."[36] He always wore the mantle of a philosopher and he seems to have remained a layman. Roman Christianity at this time was in turmoil. Christians found themselves in debate with the Jews and with various other philosophies. From an intra-ecclesial perspective, they also found themselves in debate with various "heterodox" Christian groups, e.g., the Gnostic Valentinians, the Old Testament-hating Marcionites. So, Justin's school, perhaps an early version of a Christian catechetical school, was no insular phenomenon but would have found itself in debate/dialogue/vigorous conversation with various philosophical and religious traditions. One Justin scholar, Leslie Barnard, has written that "The catechumenate did not receive definite form until c. 200 CE."[37] That may be so in respect of the classical shape of the catechumenate in the post-Constantinian era. Nevertheless, Justin must have had some program of instruction, and the program must have included key elements of Christian belief and practice.[38] That common-sense reasoning accords with the point of view of Eugene LaVerdiere, who takes it much further: "The purpose of Justin's school may . . . have been to prepare people for becoming Christians. If so, the content of the *First Apology* must reflect the teaching considered necessary for becoming a Christian in the mid-second century. Chapters 1 to 60 of the *First Apology* would thus parallel *The Didache's* instruction on the two ways (chapters 1–6) . . ."[39] This catechetical instruction would then have led up to the meaning of baptism and the Eucharist, and was surely part of Justin's project. According to Christian tradition, Justin was martyred with six of his disciples early in the reign of Marcus Aurelius, ca. 165.

Justin is probably best understood as a bridge-builder. Perhaps his key insight was that of the Logos/Word, most intensely present in Christians through initiation, and yet also seminally present in all humankind acting in accord with right reason. Justin addresses his *First Apology* to the Roman Emperor Antoninus Pius. This is more than likely simply a convention of the day acknowledging that this is an open book addressed to any interested non-Christian party. "He reached out to a non-Christian readership, confident that the reasonableness of the human mind reflected the rationality of God whether in Christian preacher or pagan reader."[40] He was the Karl Rahner, SJ of second-century Rome. If Justin represents a Rahnerian view of theology, as it were, perhaps the earliest Christian to write for a non-Christian readership,[41] one of his pupils named Tatian opted for a much more conservative version of the Christian faith, finely described by the church historian William H. C. Frend: "Where Justin was normally conciliatory, Tatian was uncompromising." We shall meet with Tatian later in chapter 5, accepting Tatian as the Syriac teacher usually known as Addai. "Where Justin saw a relative value in the pagan philosophies, Tatian saw none. . . . His acceptance after 165 of an extreme ascetic (Encratite) interpretation of Christianity involved also his rejection of the orthodox Christian moral values represented by his master Justin. He had been attracted to Christianity as a religion of protest, an effective counter to the emptiness, pride, and injustice of the Greco-Roman world as he had experienced it. He had scant use for a Christianity that was prepared even on its own terms to live with the world."[42] There never was a golden age free of crisis and the struggle towards the truth in the history of the Christian tradition. As the contemporary Dominican Timothy Radcliffe, OP is fond of pointing out, crisis is the "specialité de la maison."[43]

Some might wonder, "What about the Bishop of Rome?" Would he not have been able to deal effectively with the Gnostics, the Marcionites, and the Tatians of this world? The fact of the matter is, however, that we have so little evidence for the early to mid-second century in terms of the papacy. The consensus of historians and theologians is that the monarchical episcopate, the government of the local church by a single bishop as distinct from a group of presbyter-bishops, did not emerge with real clarity in Rome until the mid-second century. Probably until then there had been a number of house churches with a presbyter-bishop, each in communion with other presbyter-bishops, and with a "sense" of a primary house-bishop.[44] That very nicely takes us to the celebration of the Eucharist in mid-second-century Rome, and in particular to the account of Justin.

The Eucharist

Justin provides us with two accounts of the Eucharist, the fullest descriptions we have for the second century. In his *First Apology* chapter 65 there is an account of the Eucharist for the newly baptized, and in chapter 67 we find his account of the normal Sunday Eucharist. It seems to be the case that certainly by Justin's time, the mid-second century, the conjunction of the agape/community meal and the Eucharist was no longer in place. This remains something of a disputed issue among historians of the liturgy and need not be of great concern to us here.[45]

We cannot be certain when the Eucharist was celebrated, morning or evening. It may have been in the morning since Justin tells us that it was celebrated "on the day called Sunday," and we do know that Roman days ran from midnight to midnight, unlike the Jewish custom of from sunset to sunset. We do not know how the baptismal Eucharist actually began because the Christian community is already assembled by the time the neophyte is introduced to them. There are no churches in the sense of separate buildings as we have them today and as they flourished after the Edict of Milan. Churches are house-churches; that is, assemblies in someone's home. Baptism would have occurred elsewhere. As Eugene LaVerdiere helpfully comments, "Baptism and the Eucharist were celebrated in two different places. Baptism required water, normally flowing water. In Rome, this meant a pool for water from an aqueduct, such as the basin of a fountain with fresh, clean water."[46] Obviously, those who conducted the baptism had to bring the newly-baptized to the house-church where the already-baptized had assembled for the Eucharist.

Here are the texts, putting both accounts of the Eucharist together:[47]

> 65.1 After we have thus baptized him who has believed and has given his assent, we take him to those who are called brethren where they are assembled, to make common prayers earnestly for ourselves and for him who has been enlightened and for all others everywhere, that, having learned the truth, we may be deemed worthy to be found good citizens also in our actions and guardians of the commandments, so that we may be saved with eternal salvation. When we have ended the prayers, we greet one another with a kiss.
>
> Then bread and a cup of water and [a cup] of mixed wine are brought to him who presides over the brethren, and he takes them and sends up praise and glory to the Father of all in the name of the Son and of the Holy Spirit, and gives thanks at some length that we have been deemed worthy of these things from him. When he has finished the prayers and the thanksgiving, all the people give their assent by saying "Amen." ("Amen" is the Hebrew for "So be it.")
>
> And when the president has given thanks and all the people have assented, those whom we call deacons give to each of those present a portion of the bread and wine and water over which thanks have been given, and take them for those who are not present.
>
> 66.1 And we call this food "thanksgiving"; and no one may partake of it unless he is convinced of the truth of our teaching, and has been cleansed with the washing for forgiveness of sins and regeneration, and lives as Christ handed down.
>
> But we do not perceive these things as common bread or common drink; but just as our Savior Jesus Christ, being incarnate through the word of God, took flesh and blood for our salvation,

so too we have been taught that the food over which thanks have been given by a word of prayer which is from him, [the food] from which our flesh and blood are fed by transformation, is both the flesh and blood of that incarnate Jesus.

For the apostles in the records composed by them which are called Gospels, have handed down thus what was commanded of them: that Jesus took bread, gave thanks, and said, "Do this for the remembrance of me; this is my body"; and likewise he took the cup, gave thanks, and said "This is my blood"; and gave to them alone.

And the evil demons have imitated this and handed it down to be done also in the mysteries of Mithras. For as you know or may learn, bread and a cup of water are used with certain formulas in their rites of initiation.

67.1 And thereafter we continually remind one another of these things. Those who have the means help all those in need; and we are always together.

And we bless the Maker of all things through his Son Jesus Christ and through the Holy Spirit over all that we offer.

And on the day called Sunday an assembly is held in one place of all who live in town or country, and the records of the apostles or the writings of the prophets are read as time allows.

Then, when the reader has finished, the president in a discourse admonishes and exhorts [us] to imitate these good things.

Then we all stand up together and send up prayers; and as we said before, when we have finished praying, bread and wine and water are brought up, and the president likewise sends up prayers and thanksgivings to the best of his ability, and the people assent, saying the Amen; and the [elements over which] thanks have been given are distributed, and everyone partakes; and they are sent through the deacons to those who are not present.

And the wealthy who so desire give what they wish, as each chooses; and what is collected is deposited with the president.

He helps orphans and widows, and those who through sickness or any other cause are in need, and those in prison, and strangers sojourning among us; in a word, he takes care of all those who are in need.

And we assemble together on Sunday, because it is the first day, on which God transformed darkness and matter, and made the world; and Jesus Christ our Savior rose from the dead on that day; for they crucified him the day before Saturday; and the day after Saturday, which is Sunday, he appeared to his apostles and disciples, and taught them these things which we have presented to you also for your consideration.

I never cease to be thrilled by this remarkable account of the Eucharist in Justin. It is substantially, structurally, and theologically identical with the celebration of the Eucharist in our time. The one who leads in the celebration of the Eucharist is described as "the president," in Greek *ho proestos*. Contextually this refers to what we might call the bishop or the priest. Justin, like the New Testament authors, does not use the word "priest" of the Christian leader, probably to underline the distinction between the omnipresent pagan priests and Christian leaders.

One of the first things to strike us in these extracts from Justin is the place of "assent." The newly baptized person has "given assent." All the Christian people in the eucharistic assembly give their assent at the end of the eucharistic prayer by saying "Amen," something that Justin mentions twice. What is striking about this is not that it is some kind of external assent, as it were, to what is going on in baptism or the Eucharist, but that it is a fulsome entrance into those sacramental realities. The individual Christian is not so much saying, "Yes, I agree with this," as through this assent submitting to and so participating in these grace-filled sacramental realities. In today's terms we might refer to this as the "full, conscious, and active participation" in the liturgy called for, by way of example, in Vatican II's "Constitution on the Sacred Liturgy" par. 10. The liturgy is understood as how the Triune God is divinizing the Christian assembly and how that assembly acknowledges, responds, and submits to this process of being en-graced. When the newly-baptized is brought into the eucharistic assembly, we are told, prayers are offered for the assembly, the neophyte, and for *all people*. Immediately, we recognize in Justin's phrase "for all others everywhere" an illustration of his apologetic motive, demonstrating that far from being subversive Christianity is concerned with the welfare of all. *All* are prayed for. As well as this immediate apologetic motive, however, may we not see here an echo of Vatican II's "Constitution on the Church," par. 1, in which it is affirmed that the church is a sacrament of union with God and of union with "all others everywhere," to use Justin's terms? The church is not an insular enclave of the saved, but an ensign to the nations, a sacrament of salvation proclaiming and effecting God's invitation to Divine Communion to all humankind. This way of thinking also fits perfectly with Justin's notion of the Logos at work in all. The kiss of peace follows, the liturgical gesture that gives expression to our incorporation into Christ. The location of the gesture is different from our present arrangement of the Eucharist, but the meaning is surely the same. That meaning has to do with the Lord's words about being reconciled to one's brother before offering one's gift at the altar.

The eucharistic prayer is now entered into, prayed in a Trinitarian pattern—"to the Father of all in the name of the Son and of the Holy Spirit." Again, one notices that the prayer is addressed to "the Father of *all.*" This is no pusillanimous community concerned only with itself, but is marked by a universal care for all persons. The eucharistic prayer as it unfolded was an extemporaneous prayer, "to the best of his ability," but it seems to have been according to a fairly fixed pattern. Arthur Couratin writes: "It consisted in the main of thanksgiving, so much so that, after it had been uttered, *the elements were termed 'thanked-over' or 'thanksgiving' . . .*"[48] The very fact that the elements were thus described suggests that there must have been some fundamental pattern of "giving thanks." When the president has finished the prayers and the thanksgiving the people respond with "Amen." In other words, the president alone speaks the eucharistic prayer, and the congregation finally enters into it with their assent, their participatory submission to the Father's gracious action.

Holy Communion follows, with the deacons—"the only technical name Justin gives for any minister"[49]—taking Communion to those who are unable to be physically present at the celebration. It is clear from Justin's presentation that the bread and wine are not to be thought of as "common food," but as the flesh and blood of Jesus. This is the divine power of the Word/Logos working in the Incarnation and in the Eucharist. "The Word of God gave flesh and blood to Christ; the Word of God eucharistizes the bread and wine."[50] The deacons take the eucharistic elements to those who are absent. Probably one should think not only of the elderly and those who are ill, and perhaps those in prison for their Christian faith, but also those who were unable to be present because "Sunday was not a holiday for anyone who was not self-employed."[51] The deacons probably were taking Holy Communion to the slaves who were no less members of Christ's holy body as their Christian slave-owners.

"The wealthy give what they desire, as each chooses." From this collection, this community "cash box"—the expression is that of Peter Lampe[52]—the president looks after the needs of the less well-off in the community. The cash box must have been quite substantial. Peter Lampe points out that, after his excommunication, the gift of 200,000 sesterces, a large cash amount, that Marcion had given to the Roman community was returned to him very promptly. The prompt return of such a sum of money suggests persuasively that at least that amount must have been available from the cash box.[53] One patristic commentator, Maurice Jourjon, qualifies the meaning of this collection: "The collection is not our modern offertory collection but a collection understood as a fruit of communion. God's gift to us turns us into givers to others."[54] This is hardly correct. The eucharistic assembly is *already* God's gift through Christian initiation, and regularly sustained and deepened as such through the Sunday Eucharist. They become "givers to others" through this already existing sacramental process. Yes, the collection is "a *fruit* of communion," but of a communion that is already begun and that continues to be brought to completion. Jourjon makes a fine additional comment to the effect that "The deacon seems to be regarded as a minister of God's love that rouses fraternal love in us."[55] That comment coincides with the earliest significance of the diaconate outside the New Testament, in Ignatius of Antioch.[56]

Conclusion

In a recent essay on Justin, Anglican Bishop and liturgist Colin Buchanan made the point very strongly that the historian of early Christian liturgy is like someone flying from Cairo in Egypt to the Cape in South Africa attempting to get an informed picture of the vast continent of Africa below. It is impossible. Clouds get in the way of clear vision, and when the terrain below is visibly clear one can only see what one can see. That is to say, one cannot see Africa from coast to coast with everything in between, and so one cannot provide an accurate picture of the continent from that vantage point.[57] There is something in what Bishop Buchanan is saying. Nonetheless, I would argue that there is more to the liturgy and especially the Eucharist than the craft of the liturgical historian allows for, without decrying the importance of that vocation. Of course, it is impossible to "connect all the dots" in the development of the liturgy. But neither are we in a plane looking down in a disconnected fashion from above. We are in a living tradition of liturgical and eucharistic communion. We are sharing in this tradition, not just looking at it. We are being entered into the divinization of the church for the sake of the world in this long, multi-faceted, and wondrous process that is the liturgical and eucharistic tradition. Arguably that participation gives us a "nose" for enjoying through reflection these early traditions of eucharistic worship, just as, one might say, we can have a "nose" for a good bottle of wine without necessarily being able to connect all the dots of its provenance. There is something immensely salutary, and indeed enjoyable in reading how our very ancient foremothers and forefathers in the faith celebrated the Eucharist, people like Justin in second-century Rome. Arguably we may see and smell and taste a core of Christian eucharistic identity through the centuries.

3

The Eucharistic Prayer of Hippolytus

Hippolytus' liturgy for the bishop's Eucharist is the oldest eucharistic anaphora (thanksgiving prayer) to survive apart from those in the Didache, and has been used as a model for various twentieth-century liturgical rites.

STUART G. HALL[58]

Hippolytus of Rome (ca. 170–ca. 236)

FRANK LESLIE CROSS IN his classic *The Early Christian Fathers* introduces Hippolytus as "The first member of the Roman Church to stand out as a distinct personality . . ." However, we know very little about the life of Hippolytus of Rome, and in point of fact, Cross goes on to say that "after his death the facts of his life were quickly forgotten."[59] He was a well-known presbyter in the city, a theologian of repute, and a good preacher.[60] The great Origen of Alexandria heard Hippolytus preach in Rome about 212. He seems to have had some difficulties with the various bishops of Rome during his time. He attacked Pope Zephyrinus (198/9–217) on the grounds that he was a modalist, that is to say one who believes that the Father, Son, and Holy Spirit are just temporal modes of the one God. Hippolytus's language is quite intemperate: Zephyrinus is "an ignorant and greedy man[;] . . . an ignorant man, unlearned and unskilled in the church's rules[;] . . . a receiver of bribes and a money-lover."[61] He also opposed Zephyrinus's successor, Callistus (217–22). Other factors entered into his opposition to Callistus, factors described with great frankness by the historian of the early church, S. L. Greenslade: "Manifestly, Hippolytus hated Callistus, and the formal schism was in no small measure due to his jealousy. Intellectual snobbery entered into his spite, for Zephyrinus had been no theologian and Callistus was primarily an administrator; perhaps there was some plain social snobbery too, since Callistus had been a slave."[62] He certainly took issue with what he considered Callistus's lax approach to sexual sin. The idea was still abroad that after baptism into the holy body of Christ, there should be no serious sin, and sexual sin (e.g., adultery) was regarded as serious and, therefore, beyond the pale of forgiveness. Callistus wanted the church to receive such sinners back into communion. Hippolytus shared the purist rigorism of Tertullian, the North African father of the church who espoused a strong, robust Christianity that refused to yield to human weakness and sin. Hippolytus, like Tertullian, wanted a church that was a community of saints, a perennial temptation in every age. And so, Hippolytus had himself elected Bishop of Rome in opposition to Callistus, thus becoming the first antipope. There is one further consideration. Cardinal Jean Daniélou, SJ, believed that this authority problem of Hippolytus, if we may so describe it, "represents the resistance of the ancient Roman system of government by presbyters to the development of monarchical episcopacy."[63] There is something to this. During the first one hundred and fifty years or so the Roman church had no single dominant official or bishop, as has been noted in the last chapter dealing with Justin, governance being shared by a group of elders/presbyters. This does not preclude what must be considered the realistic possibility that one of this group would have been regarded as in some sense primary, but in all probability this would have been a primacy earned through the recognition of personal qualities of leadership. In Daniélou's judgment, Hippolytus reflects this older, and in that sense, more conservative position. In this regard it may be of interest to note that Hippolytus wrote in Greek, opposed perhaps to the use of the Latin language then being encouraged by the bishops of Rome. Hippolytus was obviously a rather colorful character.

Because he was schismatic and the last significant writer of the Roman community to use Greek, the transmission of his works has been patchy. His most important work is the *Refutation of All Heresies*. His treatise, *The Apostolic Tradition*, written about 215, provides us with information on the liturgy of the Roman church, and it is in this text, "the most important source of information we possess on the liturgy of the pre-Nicene church," that we shall find his thinking about and his description of the Eucharist.[64]

Hippolytus: *The Apostolic Tradition*

A standard ecumenical introduction to the study of liturgy opens up the treatment of *The Apostolic Tradition* as follows: "The history of the transmission of this text is, to say the least, complex and fraught with difficulties."[65] This is not the place to enter into those complex and intricate difficulties. Our concern is far more limited—to generate some appreciation of the beauty of the eucharistic prayer. Following in part the ideas of Alistair Stewart-Sykes, the preference in this essay will be to view *The Apostolic Tradition* as pretty much a text that emanated from what may be called the school of Hippolytus.[66] Even so, we shall continue to refer to the text's author as "Hippolytus."

Hippolytus in fact in this text provides us with a mass of liturgical details all of which are interesting in their own right, although one scholar, perhaps tongue-in-cheek, in the Reformed tradition has recently described Hippolytus in these terms: "[He] reflects the kind of churchmanship that is overly concerned with how cheese, olives, and oil are to be blessed at the Eucharist and how the evening lamps are to be lit at Vespers. He goes into great detail, for example, on what kind of people can be admitted to the catechumenate—are they respectable? The ruling principle for Hippolytus seems to be propriety."[67] Now, it is true that Hippolytus is concerned with the range of things listed here, but to reduce his concern to the level of the socially conventional is not only to misjudge Hippolytus, but to view him through a rather bare lens of mechanical, sacramental participation. He is interested in all these things, but that is because his spirituality is not gnostic but fundamentally incarnational and sacramental. In other words, for Hippolytus these things matter because *matter* matters! Despite his partially sectarian ecclesiology Hippolytus demonstrates the centrality of and his love for the Eucharist in *The Apostolic Tradition*.

The text reflects in his words "the tradition which has remained until now." So, although it is dated to about 215, it undoubtedly witnesses to Roman practice much earlier than that, perhaps even to the time of Justin. Geoffrey Cuming is emphatic that "The eucharistic prayer of [*The Apostolic Tradition*] must not be regarded as being in any sense the official text of the thanksgiving to be used at the Sunday Eucharist in Rome c. 200, though some writers tended to give this impression."[68] He points out that later on the text says "and the bishop shall give thanks according to what we said above. It is not at all necessary for him to utter the same words as we said above, as though reciting them from memory, when giving thanks to God; but let each pray according to his ability. If indeed anyone has the ability to pray at length and with a solemn prayer, it is good. But if anyone, when he prays, offers a brief prayer, do not prevent him. Only, he must pray what is sound and orthodox."[69] In other words, the bishop is free to extemporize the eucharistic prayer as he is able, but, as one would expect from Hippolytus, there is an insistence on orthodoxy.

There are two descriptions of the Eucharist to be found in Hippolytus's *Apostolic Tradition*. One is in the context of the ordination of a bishop, and the other to do with baptism. Each one will now be presented.[70]

The Ordination Eucharist

Once the ordination has taken place, we read the following:

> *Then the deacons shall present the offering to him; and he, laying his hands on it with all the presbytery, shall say, giving thanks:*

The Lord be with you.

And all shall say:

And with your spirit.

Up with your hearts.

We have [them] with the Lord.

Let us give thanks to the Lord.

It is fitting and right.

And then he shall continue thus:

We render thanks to you, O God, through your beloved child Jesus Christ, whom in the last times you sent to us as a Savior and Redeemer and angel of your will; who is your inseparable Word, through whom you made all things, and in whom you were well pleased. You sent him from heaven into a virgin's womb; and conceived in the womb, he was made flesh and was manifested as your Son, being born of the Holy Spirit and the Virgin. Fulfilling your will and gaining for you a holy people, he stretched out his hands when he should suffer, that he might release from suffering those who have believed in you.

And when he was betrayed to voluntary suffering that he might destroy death, and break the bonds of the devil, and tread down hell, and shine upon the righteous, and fix a term, and manifest the resurrection, he took bread and gave thanks to you, saying, "Take, eat; this is my body, which shall be broken for you." Likewise also the cup, saying, "This is my blood, which is shed for you; when you do this, you make my remembrance."

Remembering therefore his death and resurrection, we offer to you the bread and the cup, giving you thanks because you have held us worthy to stand before you to administer to you.

And we ask that you would send your Holy Spirit upon the offering of your holy church; that, gathering her into one, you would grant to all who receive the holy things [to receive] the fullness of the Holy Spirit for the strengthening of faith in truth; that we may praise and glorify you through your child Jesus Christ; through whom be glory and honor to you, to the Father and the Son, with the Holy Spirit, in your holy church, both now and to the ages of ages. Amen.

Commentary

The first part of the eucharistic prayer "is marked by doctrinal emphases and phraseology characteristic of, or even peculiar to, Hippolytus."[71] In other words, if one were to have regard to the other undisputed works of Hippolytus one would find a considerable number of terminological and doctrinal similarities to this initial phase of the eucharistic prayer. The rubrics of the text read: "Then the deacons shall present the offering to him; and he, laying his hands on it with all the presbytery . . ." The phrase used here "with all the presbytery" appears to suggest some form of concelebration.[72]

After the opening dialogue the prayer proceeds with what has been rightly called "a magnificent paean of praise and thanksgiving, proclaiming the mighty acts of God in salvation history."[73] Close to the beginning of the eucharistic prayer, Christ is described as "Child" and "Angel of your will," descriptions that may seem somewhat strange to our ears. The title "Child" for our Lord occurs in early Christian literature of the first two centuries. In all probability it refers to the "Servant of God" passages in Isaiah 53, where the Greek (Septuagint) translation has the word *pais*/child for "servant of God." It thus becomes one of the oldest and most important interpretations of Christ, perhaps going back ultimately to Jesus's own self-understanding. Jesus is the suffering "Servant of God." It is probably this early understanding that lies behind Hippolytus's usage here. Talking of Christ as the angel of the Father's will is also a very early interpretation. It may be a Christological remnant or variant dating back to early Jewish traditions in Christianity. It is one of the titles given to Christ up to the fourth century.[74] It may be the case that this angel terminology finds an echo in the Roman Canon where we read: "In humble prayer we ask you, Almighty God: command that these gifts be borne by the hands of your holy Angel to your altar on high . . ." Who is the "Angel" here? Raymond Moloney, the Irish liturgical theologian, in his commentary on the contemporary eucharistic prayers (and prior to the recent revision of the English translation of the Roman Missal) pays brief but interesting attention to this question. He writes: "Various solutions have been proposed concerning the identity of this figure. *Some have even thought that the reference might be to Christ . . .*"[75] In fact, Moloney opts to interpret the Angel in terms of Revelation 8:3f; 14:18. Whatever the niceties of this kind of christological exploration, what is immediately clear from the text is its strong Trinitarian character, a century before Nicaea. The Father has sent Jesus Christ born of the Holy Spirit for human salvation.

That human salvation reaches its climax in the death and resurrection of Christ, anticipated in the Eucharist. Raymond Moloney, SJ, has captured the spirit of this part of the eucharistic prayer when he says, "It is striking that this prayer singles out more than once the freedom of Christ in his dying . . ."[76] Notice the ways in which this is expressed—"voluntary suffering," "destroy[ing] death," "break[ing] the bonds of the devil," "tread[ing] down hell," and so forth. Through his death and resurrection he overcomes all those impediments that get in the way of human flourishing. As Hippolytus describes these impediments, he also uses a clause "fix a term." This phrase "fix a term" is a strange one. What does it mean? Scholarly commentators offer a variety of possible interpretations.[77] None of those which I have read is especially illuminating. Perhaps the context of the phrase is enough to provide a generic meaning. The context is one clearly of defeating evil, of overcoming death, of celebrating the resurrection through the Eucharist. "Fix a term" may be nothing more than a poetic parallel phrase, in line with Hebrew and early Christian poetic style, denoting the end of evil and destruction and the beginning of new life in Christ.

"And we ask that you would send your Holy Spirit upon the offering of your holy church . . ." This is a form of epiclesis, invoking the Holy Spirit. Because the doctrine of the divinity of the Holy Spirit does not emerge with real clarity until the fourth century, especially in the Council of Constantinople in 381, some scholars have thought that this clause may be an interpolation. However, Jasper and Cuming comment helpfully in this regard: "The Spirit is not asked to change the elements (as he surely would have been in the fourth century), but only to come upon them for the benefit of the communicants, which is not at all incongruous with the early third century."[78]

The Baptismal Eucharist

And then the offering shall be brought up by the deacons to the bishop: and he shall give thanks over the bread for the representation, which the Greeks call "antitype," of the body of Christ; and after the cup mixed with wine for the antitype, which the Greeks call "likeness," of the blood which was shed for all who believed in him;

[and] over milk and honey mixed together in fulfillment of the promise which was made to the fathers, in which he said, "a land flowing with milk and honey"; in which also Christ gave his flesh, through which those who believe are nourished like little children, making the bitterness of the heart sweet by the gentleness of his word; and over water, as an offering to signify the washing, that the inner man also, which is the soul, may receive the same thing as the body. And the bishop shall give a reason for all these things to those who receive.

And when he breaks the bread, in distributing fragments to each, he shall say:

The bread of heaven in Christ Jesus.

And he who receives shall answer: Amen.

And if there are not enough presbyters, the deacons also shall hold the cups, and stand by in good order and reverence: first, he who holds the water; second, the milk; third, the wine. And they who receive shall taste of each thrice, he who gives it saying: In God the Father almighty.

And he who receives shall say: Amen.

And in the Lord Jesus Christ. [*And he shall say:* Amen.]

And in the Holy Spirit and the holy church.

And he shall say: Amen.

So shall it be done with each one.

Commentary

"He shall give thanks" is not perhaps a bold enough translation. The Greek verb is *eucharistein,* and what of course it means at a very basic level is "to give thanks", but it means so much more than that. The translation offered by Dom Gregory Dix seems closer to the mark. He translates "he shall give thanks" as "he shall *eucharistize."* While that sounds a little cumbersome, it is preferable in our context.[79]

The words "antitype" and "likeness" are used of the eucharistic gifts to signify the realism of the identity between the bread and the wine and the body and blood of Christ, but avoiding any crude literalness. The language is not intended to be a fully thought-out articulation of the meaning of sacrament. It is for Hippolytus a "good enough" language to express his traditional eucharistic faith.

It is noteworthy that at this baptismal Eucharist there are three cups—water, milk and honey, wine—and each cup symbolizes washing, the promised land flowing with milk and honey, and the blood of Christ. It seems to be the case that the communicant, receiving the three cups, responds to a Trinitarian liturgical formula "In God the Father almighty, and in the Lord Jesus Christ, and in the Holy Spirit and the holy church." We know from both Tertullian (*Against Marcion* 1.14) and Clement of Alexandria (*Pedagogue* 1.6) of the custom of giving newly baptized Christians milk and honey, testifying to probably a widespread practice. It would seem that after communion of the bread and before communion of the cup there took place a drinking of water and then of milk mixed with honey. Milk and honey were the food of the newborn, appropriate for those newborn in Christ. Milk and honey also suggest, as Hippolytus notes, the promised land, and the new Christians have entered into that promised land through the sacraments of initiation. Hippolytus goes on to add his own contribution to the symbolism of the milk and honey: milk represents the Christ's flesh and the honey his gentleness.

Conclusion

It is a good thing with the scholars equipped for the task to probe the traditions and alliances and liturgical trajectories that lie behind the "The Apostolic Tradition." It is a good thing to read these ancient eucharistic prayers for their own sake, or better for our own sake. Meditating with these ancient

Christian prayers can help bring about a renewal of our own prayer patterns, and indeed, help to deepen our appreciation of our eucharistic bond across the centuries. Recognition of this eucharistic bond is in part what lay behind adapting the eucharistic prayer from Hippolytus's Eucharist for the ordination of a bishop in Eucharistic Prayer II in the Roman Missal. Among this great cloud of witnesses sharing our eucharistic bond over the centuries, then, stands Hippolytus, "warts and all." His eucharistic witness invites us to become "the apostolic tradition" to the coming generations of Christians.

4

The Eucharistic Prayer of Sarapion

The prayers of Sarapion provide for us what is very likely the earliest liturgical prayer for the specific blessing of oil for the sick, as well as other related elements, which may have been taken home for us by the faithful from the Sunday Eucharist.

MAXWELL E. JOHNSON[80]

THE DIDACHE WITH ITS eucharistic prayer seems to have its provenance in Syria towards the end of the first century, while the Syriac eucharistic prayer of Addai and Mari clearly comes from the same basic region and it too is before the Council of Nicaea in 325 AD. If Antioch is the flourishing center of Christianity in Syria, Alexandria is the center for Christian Egypt. The strange thing is, however, that "We have no pre-Nicene text of the eucharistic prayer from Egypt."[81] That makes the Euchologion (or Prayer Book) of Sarapion of Thmuis with its eucharistic prayer the earliest extant Egyptian example of the genre. As the opening comment of Maxwell Johnson indicates, this prayer book of Sarapion shows clearly the bridge between public worship and domestic ritual and prayer. The sacred action of the Eucharist, with all its attended elements, embraced the faithful in such a way that their own prayer/ritual at home flowed both from and to the central worship action of the community. In this instance the faithful blessed and anointed their ill sisters and brothers with oil blessed at the community Eucharist.

Sarapion was Bishop of Thmuis, a large city in the Nile Delta from about 339 A.D. He was a good friend of St. Athanasius of Alexandria.

Before he became Bishop of Thmuis he had been a monk and a companion of St. Antony of Egypt. In Antony's will he left one of his sheepskin coats to Athanasius and the other to Sarapion. Sarapion authored a number of theological works, including a Sacramentary that includes this eucharistic prayer we are about to study. Sarapion's prayer book has been thoroughly studied by the Notre Dame liturgical theologian, Maxwell E. Johnson, in his published doctoral thesis *The Prayers of Sarapion of Thmuis*.[82] Our interest here is not in the entire sacramentary, but in the eucharistic prayer. In the conclusion of his study Johnson lends support to the tentative suggestion of the Anglican liturgical theologian, Geoffrey J. Cuming, "that the prayers of Sarapion are a collection compiled from different strata or sub-groups of prayers reflecting diverse euchological sources and, hence, different authors."[83] As Cuming and Johnson develop it, the suggestion makes very good sense and is persuasive, but it does not affect as such the theological integrity of the anaphora as we now have it.

There is a somewhat classic *bon mot* of Louis Bouyer about this anaphora. He writes: "We find in it a curious mixture of Johannine imagery, tending towards a kind of harmless Gnosticism and a vaguely mystagogical philosophical jargon which was already present in Clement of Alexandria in the preceding century . . ."[84] Bouyer is quite right to recognize the Johannine emphasis on light in the eucharistic prayer. Since Alexandria and Egypt were the very heartland of Christian Gnosticism, there may linger in the prayer some elements of what he calls a "harmless Gnosticism." I would take issue personally with his language that there is in the prayer "a vaguely mystagogical philosophical jargon." I would prefer to describe the language as mystagogical Trinitarianism, so that the linguistic expression of Sarapion is less weighted in terms of philosophy and more in terms of sacramental mystagogy. In all probability, the text may be dated approximately to the mid-fourth century.[85]

Once upon a time the great twentieth-century systematic theologian Karl Rahner, SJ wrote these interesting words about theology and revelation:

> If and in so far as theology is man's reflexive self-expression about himself in the light of divine revelation, we could propose the thesis that theology cannot be complete until it appropriates the arts as an integral moment of theology itself. One could take the position that what comes to expression in a Rembrandt painting or a Brückner symphony is so inspired and borne by divine revelation, by grace and by God's self-communication, that they communicate something about what the human really is in the

eyes of God, which cannot be completely translated into verbal theology.[86]

Now a fourth-century Egyptian anaphora is neither a Rembrandt painting nor a Brückner symphony, but arguably one might describe it as poetry. As poetry perhaps this anaphora may communicate "something about what the human really is in the eyes of God" in a way that theology-in-prose does not. Anyway, that will be the perspective taken in this reflection on Sarapion's anaphora. It is poetry and a theological reading should approach it as such. Let's read the poem first.

The Eucharistic Prayer

It is fitting and right to praise, to hymn, to glorify you, the uncreated Father of the only-begotten Jesus Christ.

We praise you, uncreated God, unsearchable, ineffable, incomprehensible by all created being.

We praise you who are known by the only-begotten Son, who were spoken of through him and interpreted and made known to created nature.

We praise you who know the Son and reveal to the saints the glories about him, who are known by your begotten Word, and seen and interpreted to the saints.

We praise you, unseen Father, provider of immortality: you are the fountain of life, the fountain of light, the fountain of all grace and all truth, lover of man and lover of the poor; you reconcile yourself to all and draw all to yourself through the coming of your beloved Son.

We pray, make us living men.

Give us a spirit of light, that we may know you, the true (God) and him whom you have sent, Jesus Christ.

Give us Holy Spirit, that we may be able to speak and expound your unspoken mysteries.

May the Lord Jesus Christ and the Holy Spirit speak in us and hymn you through us.

For you are above every principality and power and virtue and dominion and every name that is named, not only in this age but in the age to come.

Beside you stand thousands of thousands and myriads of myriads of angels, archangels, thrones, dominions, principalities, and powers. Beside you stand the two most honorable seraphim with six wings, and the feet with two, and fly with two; and they cry, "Holy." With them receive also our cry of "Holy," as we say: "Holy, Holy, Holy, Lord of Sabaoth; heaven and earth are full of your glory."

Full is heaven, full also is earth of your excellent glory, Lord of the powers. Fill also this sacrifice with your power and your partaking; for to you we offered this living sacrifice, this bloodless offering.

To you we offered this bread, the likeness of the body of the only-begotten. [This bread is the likeness of the holy body.] For the Lord Jesus Christ, in the night when he was betrayed, took bread, broke it, and gave it to his disciples, saying, "Take and eat; this is my body which is broken for you for forgiveness of sins." Therefore we also offered the bread, making the likeness of the death.

We beseech you through this sacrifice: be reconciled to us all and be merciful, O God of truth. And as this bread was scattered over the mountains, and was gathered together and became one, so gather your holy Church out of every nation and every country and every city and village and house, and make one living Catholic Church.

We offered also the cup, the likeness of the blood. For the Lord Jesus Christ after supper took a cup and said to his disciples, "Take, drink; this is the new covenant, which is my blood of the shed for you for forgiveness of sins." Therefore we also offered the cup, presenting the likeness of the blood.

Let your holy Word come on this bread, O God of truth, that the bread may become body of the Word; and on this cup, that the cup may become blood of the Truth; and make all who partake receive a medicine of life for the healing of every disease, and for the empowering of all advancement and virtue; not for condemnation, O God of truth, nor for censure and reproach.

For we have called upon you, the uncreated, through the only-begotten in Holy Spirit. Let this people receive mercy; let it be counted worthy of advancement; let angels be sent out to be present among the people for bringing to naught the evil one, and for establishing of the church.

And we entreat also for all who have fallen asleep, of whom is also the remembrance.

After the recitation of the names: Sanctify these souls, for you know them all; sanctify all [the souls] that are fallen asleep in the Lord and number them among all your holy powers, and give them a place and a mansion in your kingdom.

Receive also the thanksgiving of the people, and bless those who offered the offerings and the thanksgivings, and grant health and soundness and cheerfulness and all advancement of soul and body to all this people.

Through your only-begotten Jesus Christ in Holy Spirit; as it was and is and shall be to generations of generations and to all the ages of ages. Amen.

Reflection

Now to a few brief reflections that spring out of this anaphora-poem. The first thing we notice about this anaphora-poem is the strong note of praise in the first few sentences. "We praise you" occurs four times. Returning to some comments made in the earlier chapter on Addai and Mari, this element of praise runs throughout the entirety of the liturgy, of course, but it is only proper that it come to a particular focus here. Praise is the right ecology for growth in knowledge of God. "Praising God, recognizing him as God in feeling, word and action, is a key to the ecology in which right knowledge of God grows . . ."[87] If the Eucharist is the liturgical center of God's creative ecology, then this praising preface pulls us properly into place. That place is an expansive one. Maxwell Johnson points out that praising God expands into Christology here and then back into the praise of God once more in a kind of mystagogical pattern: "Theological praise leads into Christology, Christology leads back to praise of God *in se*, and the pattern is repeated again with its conclusion provided by the Sanctus and its introduction."[88] It can be argued that we do not make enough of praise, the praise of other human beings or the praise of God who is the ground of all being. Perhaps there is some impediment to praise rooted in our personal environments and circumstances, but without regular praise, authentic and genuine praise, human life is enormously deprived, to say nothing of what happens to us when we genuinely praise God.

The late American systematic theologian Daniel W. Hardy (1930–2007) wrote a fine essay in the mid-1980s with the title "The Systematics of

Praise." It is the only really systematic attempt of which I know to develop a comprehensive understanding of what praise is all about. Hardy writes:

> It can be seen . . . that praise is a comprehensive activity which "composes the spirit to love" (Coleridge), and does so by integrating man's capacities and his being by bringing them into a right relation with its object. It is not, however, accomplished fully in an instant. It is better seen as a self-refining activity or passion. Attention and determination give this activity its content, and are thus part of the activity of praise. But praise drives them to ever-closer discrimination of the truth of the object which is attended to and determined; praise brings their refinement through its satisfaction with, or enjoyment of, the object with which they are concerned.[89]

The passage demands close attention. At the very least in respect of our present essay we may say that the consistent praising of God especially as here in the liturgy promotes our human self-refinement and flourishing. That surely is the underlying reason why we have this repeated "We praise you" at the beginning of the anaphora.

This note of human self-refinement, satisfaction, and flourishing is given fine expression in the line: "We pray, make us living men." Immediately, one is reminded of the great sound bite from Irenaeus of Lyons, "the glory of God is the human person fully alive." That seems to me to be what Sarapion is getting at here. Through the refinement and flourishing that comes from praising God we petition God to make us "living," that is to say, people who are instinct with vitality and vibrancy, in every sense of the word. Trinitarian awareness permeates these lines also. That last line says it all—*May the Lord Jesus Christ and the Holy Spirit speak in us and hymn you through us.* The idea seems to be that we are caught up into the Trinity in our Word and Spirit praising of the Father.

The language of sacrifice figures significantly in this anaphora-poem. "To you we offered this bread. . . . We beseech you through this sacrifice. . . . We offered also the cup . . ." It is important to recognize with Maxwell Johnson that sacrifice is a polyvalent term in the patristic period. Further, it does not have any of the polemical overtones that were generated in the sixteenth century. Johnson writes: "It would be wrong to expect a clear, consistent, and detailed systematic theological treatment of the Eucharist as sacrifice in an ancient liturgical text or to assume, on the basis of the language of a classic liturgical text alone, that a clear distinction between different interpretations of 'sacrifice' is implied or intended."[90] Sacrifice may signify not only the eucharistic elements, but the entire liturgical rite, and perhaps especially the self-offering of the community. A recovered sense of a polyvalent sense of "sacrifice" is a common element in the various ecumenical dialogues on the Eucharist that have taken place since Vatican II. Recognizing this polyvalence in Sarapion may help us see that it is not new, but something long-established in liturgical practice and theological thinking.

The Sanctus and the Institution Narrative are there as we would expect. However, there is at least one thing that we probably would not expect, and that is the epiclesis of the Word. "Let your holy Word come on this bread, O God of truth, that the bread may become body of the Word . . ." What one would expect in this context is an epiclesis of the Holy Spirit. What we have is an epiclesis of the Word. Liturgical scholars continue to debate the significance of this, and in terms of liturgical scholarship that debate must go on. At the same time, it seems legitimate from the point of view of systematic theology to insist that where the Word is the Spirit is, and where the Spirit is the Word is. In a Trinitarian ecology how could it be different?

There are also some interesting emphases in the prayers. "Make all who partake to receive a medicine of life for the healing of every disease, and for the empowering of all advancement and virtue; not for condemnation, O God of truth, nor for censure and reproach." We recognize right away, beginning in Ignatius of Antioch, the notion that the Eucharist is the "medicine of immortality." The Eucharist makes us whole and complete. The image of God lying behind these lines does not have to do with condemnation, or censure, or reproach. This is the God who will make us "living men," healed of everything that hinders us presently from the Communion of Love that is God.

"Let angels be sent out to be present among the people . . ." Do angels exist? "No!" says Bernard Cooke: "We don't need a bridge to God, God is with us. Very truly heaven is here. . . . If heaven is being with God, we already are with God, unless we refuse to accept the friendship offered us through Christ."[91] Cooke's affirmation of the immanent presence of God renders angels redundant. Angels may have been necessary when humankind entertained an excessively transcendent or monarchical concept of God. With a more organic sense of God, with God present in and to all of creation and especially his human creatures, we no longer need angels.

Do we need angels? "Yes!" says John Macquarrie: "The doctrine of the angels opens our eyes to this vast, unimaginable cooperative striving and service, as all things seek to be like God and to attain to fullness of being in him. . . . The panorama of creation must be far more breath-taking than we can guess in our corner of the cosmos."[92] Perhaps in disallowing angels Bernard Cooke is entertaining a God who is too frugal, who is parsimonious as creator. But if God is as God is manifest in the New Testament, the One who generously lets-be all that is, angels may exemplify something of the extent of God's unending creative generosity. At the very least we may say that angels signify God's healing and loving presence among his people. Asking them to be sent out is finally asking God so to be present in our midst, and paradigmatically in the Eucharist, that he will transform us into communion in God's own Trinitarian self.

When we come at the anaphora in this "poetic" way we are led mystagogically further and further into an awareness of our eucharistic God.

Conclusion

Liturgists accept the responsibility in all the churches and Christian communities of preparing and, at times, drawing up forms of worship that will speak to our contemporaries. It is salutary for them, and indeed for all of us, to read slowly and meditatively some of these ancient eucharistic prayers. The quality of their praying can only enhance the quality of our praying. Re-newing our lives of worship and prayer does not mean always creating novel forms. Remaining in prayer and worship with earlier generations, in the communion of saints, does not mean slavishly imitating them. But it surely does mean learning from them, even as we continue to worship and pray with them. Therein lies the importance of Sarapion.

5

Eucharistic Prayer of Addai and Mari

Among the elements in the eucharistic prayer of Addai and Mari were a Sanctus unit and an invocation of the Holy Spirit on the bread and wine, but apparently not a narrative of institution . . .

PAUL F. BRADSHAW AND MAXWELL E. JOHNSON[93]

IN 2008 THE HISTORIAN Philip Jenkins published a very fine book entitled *The Lost History of Christianity*.[94] The book does what its title suggests, that is, it plots the history and development of Christianity in the Middle East, Africa, and Asia, a history about which most Latin/Roman/Western Christians know almost nothing. We Latin or Roman or Western Christians tend to think of the church only from a Western point of view, a point of view that is much too Eurocentric and/or North American. We are very unfamiliar with the geography, history, and theology of the church as it took root in other parts of the world. Philip Jenkins seeks to correct that. One of the areas that he explores in his book is the Syriac-speaking church, and he offers a rich historical background for approaching the Anaphora of Addai and Mari, our concern in this chapter. The Liturgy of Saints Addai and Mari originated in Edessa, a city of northeastern Syria near the frontier between the Roman Empire and Persia. Addai was the traditional apostle of Edessa and Mari was his disciple. Edessa was a vibrant, early center of Christianity.

The Anaphora of Addai and Mari[95]

The Liturgy of Addai and Mari was composed in Syriac, a dialect of the Aramaic language and very close to the language that Jesus himself spoke. The earliest texts of the anaphora are simply entitled "The Sanctification of the Apostles." Addai was the traditional founder of the church at Edessa; Mari was his disciple, but in terms of verifiable history we know very little about them. Addai has been identified with Tatian (ca 160), the most famous or perhaps infamous pupil of Justin Martyr (ca. 160), whom we considered earlier.

The University of Cambridge New Testament scholar and Orientalist, Francis Crawford Burkitt (1864–1935), hypothesized that Addai was in fact a form of the name Tatian, Justin's pupil. If *Addai* were the same as *Tatian,* argued Burkitt, "it would afford a simple solution of a historical difficulty, which is, that the Syriac-speaking Christians preserved the tradition that 'Addai' brought the Diatessaron to their land, but do not seem to have heard of 'Tatian' except from the Greek writer Eusebius."[96] Although the issue remains debated and it is hardly of great historical importance, I find myself convinced by Burkitt. Addai is Tatian. It's interesting to note that Burkitt now finds himself re-discovered in an intriguing book by Janet Soskice about two sisters, Agnes and Margaret Smith, who were responsible for discovering a number of important manuscripts, including Syriac manuscripts, in the monastery of St. Catherine's on Sinai. Apparently, the scholarly Burkitt accompanied the two ladies on one of their expeditions.[97]

Enough about peripheral issues! Let's get down to reading the text of the anaphora:

Priest: Peace be with you.

Response: And with your spirit.

Priest: The grace of our Lord Jesus Christ and the love of God the Father, and the fellowship of the Holy Spirit be with us all, now and at all times and forever and ever.

Response: Amen.

Priest: Let your hearts be on high.

Response: They are with you, O God.

Priest: The offering is offered to God, the Lord of all.

Answer: It is fitting and right.

Deacon: Peace be with us.

Priest: Worthy of praise from every mouth and thanksgiving from every tongue is the adorable and glorious name of the Father and of the Son and of the Holy Spirit. He created the world through his grace and its inhabitants in his loving-kindness; he redeemed men through his mercy, and dealt very graciously with mortals.

Your Majesty, O Lord, a thousand thousand heavenly beings adore; myriad myriads of angels, and ranks of spiritual beings, ministers of fire and spirit, together with the holy cherubim and seraphim, glorify your name, crying out and glorifying, unceasingly calling to one another and saying:

Response: Holy, holy, holy is the Lord God Almighty; heaven and earth are full of his glory. Hosanna in the highest! Hosanna to the Son of David! Blessed is he who has come and comes in the name of the Lord. Hosanna in the highest!

Priest: And with these heavenly hosts we, also even we, your lowly, weak, and miserable servants, Lord, give you thanks because you have dealt very graciously with us in a way which cannot be repaid. For you put on our human nature to give us life through your divine nature; you raised us from our lowly state; you restored our fallen state, and resurrect our mortality, and forgive our sins, and acquit our sinfulness, and enlighten our understanding, and, our Lord and our God, you conquered our enemies, and give victory to the unworthiness of our frail nature in the overflowing mercies of thy grace.

And for all your helps and graces towards us, let us raise to you praise and honor and thanksgiving and adoration, now and ever and world without end.

Response: Amen.

Deacon: Pray in your hearts. Peace be with us.

Priest: You, Lord, through your many mercies which cannot be told, be graciously mindful of all the pious and righteous fathers who were pleasing in your sight, in the commemoration of the body and blood of your Christ, which we offer to you on the pure and holy altar, as you taught us.

And grant us your tranquility and your peace for all the days of this age.

Response: Amen.

Priest: That all the inhabitants of the earth may know you, that you alone are the true God and Father, and you sent our Lord Jesus Christ, your beloved Son, and he, our Lord and Our God, taught us through his life-giving gospel all the purity and holiness of the prophets, apostles, martyrs, confessors, bishops, priests, deacons, and all the children of the holy catholic Church who have been sealed with the living seal of holy baptism.

And we also, Lord, your lowly, weak, and miserable servants, who have gathered and stand before you, and have received through tradition the example which is from you, rejoicing, glorifying, exalting, commemorating, and celebrating this great mystery of the passion, death and resurrection of our Lord Jesus Christ.

May your Holy Spirit, Lord, come and rest on this offering of your servants, and bless and sanctify it, that it may be to us, Lord, for the pardon of sins and for the forgiveness of shortcomings, and for the great hope of resurrection from the dead, and new life in the kingdom of heaven, with all who have been pleasing in your sight.

And because of all your wonderful dispensation towards us, with open mouths and uncovered faces we give you thanks and glorify you without ceasing in your Church, which has been redeemed by the precious blood of your Christ, offering up praise, honor, thanksgiving and adoration to your living and holy and life-giving name, now and at all times forever and ever.

Response: Amen.

Commentary

Immediately we recognize in the dialogue leading into the eucharistic prayer something very similar to our own experience of the celebration. This is especially the case with the following words: "Let your hearts be on high" along with the response "They are with you, O God"; again, "The offering is offered to God, the Lord of all" along with the response "It is fitting and right." As the dialogue opens the eucharistic prayer proper, it composes our minds and hearts for this great prayer of thanksgiving. In a similar fashion the following part of the prayer is almost identical both in tone and at times in words to a typical preface in the Roman Missal: there is an emphasis on praise "from every mouth" and on thanksgiving "from every tongue." This element of praise runs throughout the entirety of the liturgy, of course, but it is only proper that it comes to a particular focus here. Praise, as we have recognized, is the right ecology for growth in knowledge of God. "Praising God, recognizing him as God in feeling, word, and action is a key to the ecology in which right knowledge of God grows . . ."[98] If the Eucharist is the liturgical center of God's creative ecology, then this praising preface pulls us properly into place.

The *Sanctus* now takes place: "Holy, holy, holy is the Lord God Almighty; heaven and earth are full of his glory. Hosanna in the highest!" It is certainly interesting given that the new translation of the Roman Missal makes the transition from "Lord God of power and might" to "Lord God of hosts" that this ancient eucharistic prayer does not immediately speak of "hosts/angels." I have checked the Syriac text, and it says "Almighty," not "hosts."[99] Nonetheless, the context is very clear that we are conjoined with the angels in the praise of God. The anaphora goes on to say "And with these heavenly hosts . . ." Of course, the *Sanctus* has its Scriptural origins in Isaiah 6:3, the song of the seraphim, and although we are unable to trace its exact and precise origins in the development and the history of the liturgy, its sheer antiquity as here in Addai and Mari and its theological meaning give the *Sanctus* a sense of power and sublimity. Think, for example, of the magnificent description of the hymn in the words of theologian Rudolf Otto: "I have heard the Sanctus, Sanctus, Sanctus of the cardinals in St. Peter's, the Swiat, Swiat, Swiat in the Kreml Cathedral, and the Hagios, Hagios, Hagios of the patriarch in Jerusalem. In whatever language they resound, these most sublime words that have come from human lips always grip one in the depth of the soul, with a mighty shudder, exciting and calling into play the mystery of the otherworldly latent therein."[100] Clearly, Otto's "idea of the holy angels" has a marvelous sweep to it, a sweep that is both existential and cosmic.

The angels/the Sanctus in the liturgy helps to keep our liturgy rightly focused in a God-ward direction. This has been welcomed by the reformed theologian Gabriel Fackre when he says, "Interests that run from the therapeutic to the political have so intruded themselves into our Sunday services that the theocentrism of Isaiah's temple has disappeared."[101] The angels in the anaphora of Addai and Mari and the return of the angels in the new translation help us, if such help is needed, to re-orient our liturgy in a more theocentric direction.

It is, indeed, this theocentric direction of the liturgy that enables me to enter more fully into some language used in the anaphora that would not occur to me spontaneously. I mean here such language as this: "we, your lowly, weak, and miserable servants . . .", language that is in fact repeated a second time in the anaphora. One part of me does not especially like this kind of language because it seems to reduce humankind to a very low status. On the other hand, it really is no more than a particular way of expressing the human condition in the presence of the Divine. Think, for example, of the Anglican priest/poet George Herbert's wonderful poem *Love III*. In that poem Herbert shows himself aware as a communicant coming into God's presence in the eucharistic banquet:

> *Love bade me welcome,*
> *yet my soul drew back guilty of dust and sin . . .*

In the presence of Divine Love the human person recognizes the self as most unlovely. It would be extremely difficult, even impossible, not to agree with Herbert's sentiments.[102] In reality, it seems to me that is all that Addai and Mari intend by this language of lowliness, weakness, and misery.

The final aspect of this anaphora to which I want to draw attention is the epiclesis, "May your Holy Spirit, Lord, come and rest on this offering of your servants, and bless and sanctify it, that it may be to us, Lord, for the pardon of sins and for the forgiveness of shortcomings, and for the great hope of resurrection from the dead, and new life in the kingdom of heaven, with all who have been pleasing in your sight." One of the great retrievals of the liturgical renewal consequent upon Vatican II and, indeed, in other Christian eucharistic prayers was the re-discovery of the epiclesis in the eucharistic prayer. The epiclesis is "an invocation of the Father that he send the Holy Spirit to transform the gifts which the church brings before him."[103] The Holy Spirit transforms the gifts of bread and wine into the body and blood of Jesus Christ so that through our participation we too may be transformed. The epiclesis in Addai and Mari has to do with the forgiveness of sins and shortcomings so that we may be enfolded in the Resurrection and the communion of the saints. The theology of this antique epiclesis and of our contemporary epicleses is coincident.

The Institution Narrative

Thus far what has been said about the Anaphora of Addai and Mari will not pose any significant challenge to the reflective reader. This may change when it is recognized that the anaphora does not contain the Institution Narrative. Simply put, when we read through the anaphora we do not find one. The distinguished historian of Armenian liturgy, Gabriele Winkler, made the following opening comment in an essay published in 2004: "After many years of unquestioned certainty that all anaphoras contained the Institution Narrative . . . there is a general consensus today that not all Eucharistic formularies contained the Institution Narrative, the main witness being Addai and Mari."[104] In this statement she is claiming that there is a general agreement among the liturgical/historical scholars that not all eucharistic prayers from Christian antiquity contained the narrative of the Last Supper in which we find the eucharistic words: "Take and eat, this is my body," etc. For most Western Christians, and especially Roman Catholics, this is very strange and perhaps even astonishing. We are so accustomed to the centrality of the Institution Narrative in the eucharistic prayer, at the center of which are the words of consecration, that the absence of these words in a very ancient eucharistic prayer is, to say the least, most challenging.

While some scholars are of the opinion that the narrative including the eucharistic words of Jesus were somehow omitted from Addai and Mari, "The consensus of the latest scholarship is that *Addai and Mari* in its original form never included the Institution Narrative."[105] These are the words of the greatest living Catholic historian of Orthodox liturgy, Robert Taft, SJ. He is in agreement with Gabriele Winkler. Taft, however, goes on to make the point that we can be too literal and wooden-headed in our approach to the eucharistic words. This is what he writes: "Though *Addai and Mari* may not cite the words of institution literally, it contains them virtually, in explicit references to the eucharistic institution, to the Last Supper, to the body and blood and sacrifice of Christ and to the oblation of the church, thereby clearly demonstrating the intention of repeating what Jesus did in obedience to his command, 'Do this in memory of me.'"[106] Referring to the *General Instruction on the Roman Missal* (1969, paragraph 54) and to the *Catechism of the Catholic Church* (paragraph 1352) he goes on to say: "Catholic teaching of late has moved toward the broader view that the eucharistic consecration comprises the prayer over the gifts in its entirety."[107] This is the perspective from which the Catholic Church has come to recognize in 2002 the validity of this eucharistic prayer that does not contain the Institution Narrative including the eucharistic words of Jesus. It is more than the straightforward recognition that this eucharistic prayer from Christian antiquity may be regarded as valid by Roman Catholic Christians. The prayer, in point of fact, continues to be used by the Chaldean Church, especially in Iran and Iraq. What the Vatican did was to recognize that the Institution Narrative is virtually present throughout the entirety of this eucharistic prayer.[108]

This is not the place to develop the point in any detail. However, it needs to be remembered that fixing the precise moment of consecration in respect of the eucharistic words of Jesus was a phenomenon rather late in development in Christian tradition. Historically there was no attempt to define a moment of consecration before the Middle Ages, and the rise of Scholasticism with "an overriding desire for precision."[109] One example might be St. Thomas Aquinas: "Whence it must be said that if the priest utters only the aforementioned words [For this is my body] with the intention of confecting this sacrament, this sacrament will be effected; because the intention causes these words to be understood as though they were offered in Christ's person, even if the words preceding were not said."[110] Even in the Latin West, long after scholasticism had been well-established, a nuanced position about the precise moment of consecration was never entirely absent. Jacques Benigne Bossuet (1624–1707), the great exponent of post-Tridentine and baroque spirituality wrote: "The intent of liturgies and, in general, of consecratory prayers, is not to focus our attention on precise moments, but to have us attend to the action in its entirety and to its complete effect. . . . It is to render more vivid what is being done that the Church speaks at each moment as though it were accomplishing the entire action then and there, without asking whether the action has already been accomplished or is perhaps still to be accomplished."[111] Bossuet is aware of the debate that has gone on, especially between East and West, on the precise moment of consecration. His perspective is not to dwell on that precise moment but to attend to the entirety of the liturgical action. In a similar way, the French Benedictine, Dom Charles Chardon, OSB (1695–1771), writing in his 6 volume *Histoire des sacraments* in 1745 has this to say about the traditional dispute between East and West concerning the consecration:

> Despite this diversity [over the moment of consecration] there was formerly no dispute over this subject. The Greeks and Latins were convinced that the species [of bread and wine] were changed into the body and blood of our Savior in virtue of the words of

the Canon of the Mass, without examining the precise moment at which this change occurred, and not just which of the words [of the anaphora] effected it as over against other words. One side said the change was effected by the prayer and invocation of the priest; the others said that it was the result of the words of our Lord when he instituted this august sacrament. And they in no way believed that these different ways of expressing themselves were opposed to each other [and indeed they are not, as would be easy to show]. But we shall leave that to the theologians to treat.[112]

Needless to say, these theological/liturgical points of view from Bossuet and Charndon have nothing immediately to say to the missing Institution Narrative and the eucharistic words in the Anaphora of Addai and Mari. They do indicate nonetheless that closely related theological questions were not alien to the Catholic tradition of historical reflection, and therefore, that should not prove alien or alienating for traditional Christians today.

Conclusion

In respect of a conclusion to these brief reflections on Addai and Mari let us return to the magisterial Robert Taft. He himself concludes his essay on the Roman recognition of the validity of the anaphora with these words: "I consider it [the recognition of the validity of the anaphora of Addai and Mari] the most important magisterial teaching since Vatican II."[113] Very strong language indeed! It would seem that Taft means that eucharistic validity from a Roman Catholic point of view is not intrinsically and necessarily tied only to verbal formulations, but also reaches out to include intentionality. With appropriate qualifications what Taft is referring to could have implications for eucharistic traditions other than ancient or Eastern ones.

6

Baldwin of Ford and Friends

For Baldwin, the highest good and perfection to which the just are led by the Spirit is the faith that works in love. The consummation of this faith is the knowledge and love of Christ, which finds it most perfect expression in the consumption of the "bread of angels," the Word himself in his spiritual presence.

GARY MACY[114]

"BY THE END OF the twelfth century, the finger of the papacy lay on every living pulse in the church. The last pope of the century, Innocent III (1198–1216), may stand as the greatest representative of this pinnacle of papal power and influence."[115] Pope Innocent III was the pope who summoned the greatest reforming council of the Middle Ages, Lateran IV, in 1215—the council which first formally used the theological term *transubstantiation*. What few remember is that Innocent III as a young student, Lothar of Segni, had made a pilgrimage to England, to the shrine of Thomas Becket of Canterbury, described by church historian Eamon Duffy as "the great martyr for the spiritual rights of the church against the claims of secular rulers," and this issue was to be very important to the future pope.[116]

What still fewer recognize is that it was probably an Englishman, Robert Pullen, who coined the term transubstantiation, and that an Archbishop of Canterbury, Baldwin of Ford, had been responsible for a defense of the term. Twelfth-century England played an important part in the reform of the church and in the development of eucharistic theology. Our primary interest in this chapter will be Archbishop Baldwin of Ford, but it is helpful to introduce the other *dramatis personae*, especially Robert Pullen and Thomas Becket.

Cardinal Robert Pullen[117]

Robert Pullen was an English theologian and cardinal, in fact the first English cardinal, made such by Pope Lucius II (1144–45).[118] He studied at Paris under the famed William of Champeaux. Returning to England, he taught at Exeter, in Oxford, and then later in Paris.[119] When St. Bernard of Clairvaux's disciple, Bernardo Pignatelli of Pisa, became the new Cistercian Pope—the reform-minded Eugenius III—Bernard exhorted Pullen to offer to advise and support him.[120] Bernard was probably not informed in a detailed fashion about Robert's theology. Robert was not a monastic like Bernard or Eugenius III, but "as a professor he fitted into the Bernardine scheme."[121]

Robert's extant writings include some sermons and "Eight Books of Sentences," written in Oxford probably before 1142, and described by Francis Courtney as "the earliest comprehensive theological work to be produced by an English writer."[122] Courtney offers an interesting aside on these early scholastics, including Pullen: "What were exciting discoveries in their day have since become part of the common stock of ideas. They did not possess the knowledge of Aristotle available to their thirteenth century successors."[123] Aristotelian philosophy became taken for granted in later medieval theology, but for scholars like Baldwin and Robert Pullen, this was cutting edge thinking. However, St. Bernard, no friend of any theology driven by philosophy, describes Robert Pullen's theology as "sane." Robert stands in a sound tradition, is what Bernard means. His sanity in theology comes to expression particularly in two areas, his political theory and his eucharistic reflection.

In his *Sentences*, Robert discusses the "two swords" tradition of authority.[124] The church on earth has two swords: the spiritual sword given to the clergy, the temporal sword given to the laity. But both are "conferred," both are given. "The convenient passive in his verbs dispenses Pullen from stating either that the church confers the temporal sword on the secular ruler, or that the secular ruler receives his sword directly from God. . . . Pullen does not state that the secular ruler wields his sword under the church's direction, but he implies it."[125] This was a very turbulent issue in the Middle Ages. The spiritual is finally superior to the temporal. This aspect of his theology will play out fully when we turn to the second of our *dramatis personae,* Thomas Becket.

Book VIII of the *Sentences* provides, among other topics, Robert's account of the Eucharist. Francis Courtney remarks at the outset of his treatment of Pullen's eucharistic theology: "He does not use the term transubstantiation, but clearly holds this doctrine."[126] Far from that being the case, it now seems in the light of more recent research that Robert Pullen is in fact the first to use the term, and to use it in a slightly different form, *transubstantio.* Researching medieval, particularly twelfth-century manuscripts, the medievalist Joseph Goering found one in Corpus Christi College, Oxford, and one in Peterhouse, Cambridge, both using the term *transubstantio.* Goering makes an excellent, cumulative case that Robert Pullen is the theological master behind these two manuscripts, and the first to use the neologism *transubstantio,* "transubstantiation." He concludes: "The evidence taken together permits the tentative hypothesis that the term 'transubstantiation' was first introduced at Paris around 1140, and that Robert Pullen was its inventor."[127] The term, for Pullen, describes the change that takes place during the celebration of the Eucharist, from bread and wine to the body and blood of Christ. Nothing more, but nothing less is intended by *transubstantio.* In Manuscript 32 of Corpus Christi College, Oxford, Goering's supposed author, Robert Pullen, writes: "In this consecration there is no transformation of quality but, as I might put it, a transubstantiation (*transubstantio*) or transmutation of this substance into that one."[128] It had for Pullen nothing whatever to do with the philosophy of Aristotle but, rather, was his word for the eucharistic transformation witnessed throughout the tradition. The fact that he writes, "as I might put it," suggests that he realizes the novelty of the word, though not the novelty of the eucharistic conviction underlying it.

The Eucharist is the sacrifice and the salvation of the church. "The sacrifice is celebrated with this body and blood, so that the participant, whole and entire, may be vitalized by it."[129] The passion and sacrificial death of Christ is signified for Pullen by the separate reception of the elements by the priest. The very separation signifies Christ's death. "While the flesh is eaten, and the blood is poured into the mouth, the passion of the Lord is penetrated, both by the body slain and the blood outpoured."[130]

The communion of the church is built up and signified through the communion of the Eucharist: "Different grains come together to this sacrifice, since it is prepared for the different persons of the church. Many grains make together one bread, and the many persons for whom the re-making is given, are one church."[131] The Eucharist is, therefore, "the principal sacrament of the church."[132] In the context of this chapter on Baldwin of Ford the most interesting fact is that Robert Pullen was Baldwin's theology professor about 1160, and so it is reasonable to assume that the eucharistic theology of the teacher will be found in the eucharistic theology of the pupil.[133]

Archbishop Thomas Becket

Baldwin of Ford was to become, in time, the second successor of Archbishop Thomas Becket of Canterbury. In 1538, King Henry VIII issued a proclamation that everything that reminded people of St. Thomas Becket was to be destroyed, including his burial place in Canterbury Cathedral, and every mention of his name in official prayer books.

Thomas Becket, born in London in 1118, is the best-known English contemporary of Baldwin of Ford. After studies in Paris, Becket joined the household of Theobald, Archbishop of Canterbury. Data and records are incomplete, but it is very likely that one of Thomas's Parisian teachers was the same Robert Pullen who was Baldwin's teacher.[134] Theobald recognized Becket's gifts and sent him for further studies in civil and ecclesiastical law to Bologna and Auxerre, and ordained him deacon. Though Beryl Smalley maintains that "he had a patchy education," especially in matters theological, Thomas was superbly equipped in the law to serve as an emissary for both king and archbishop.[135]

It was on Archbishop Theobald's recommendation that King Henry II of England appointed Thomas chancellor of the realm. Archbishop Theobald probably hoped that the new chancellor would be the protector of the church when it came to matters of dispute with the king. He would be disappointed. The king and the chancellor became very close friends, but it would seem that Thomas was not entirely at ease in his "temporal" position as chancellor. He entered into correspondence with Abbot Peter of Celle, seeking what we would perhaps refer to as "spiritual direction." As Beryl Smalley puts it, "To receive a letter of spiritual direction from [Peter] conferred a certificate of piety."[136] Peter declined, undoubtedly because of Thomas's too "temporal" position and influence. When Theobald died, King Henry appointed his chancellor, Thomas Becket, as Archbishop of Canterbury in 1162. In that year Thomas was ordained priest, and eight days later consecrated archbishop.

It was inevitable that the former close relationship of Thomas and Henry would become difficult. "All over Europe disputes were taking place about the respective roles of king and church in appointments to bishoprics and on the subject of separate church courts."[137] Who had ultimate authority, king or church? Was the spiritual sword superior to the temporal? While the authority of the church was certainly dependent upon the king for support, and enforcement in practical matters, royal authority could hardly be said to be absolute without erasing the fundamentals of ecclesiology.

The clash between Henry and Thomas came about with regard to church courts. Thomas's resolute defense of church property (often very extensive and a huge source of income), as well as Henry's attempts to raise money by imposing taxes on the church were bound to come to conflict. Henry defended the authority of the throne, Thomas the authority of the church. Matters came to a head in 1164 when the king summoned a council of his chief advisers at Clarendon. This council issued a document, the "Constitutions of Clarendon," which set out protocols for regulating affairs between king and church. Clause 9 of the Constitutions forbade any appeal beyond the Archbishop of Canterbury's court without the royal consent. In other words, no cleric of any standing or order could appeal to Rome without the king's permission.

Thomas finally refused to accept these protocols, was tried before the king, and almost condemned for treason. The net result was Thomas going into exile for six years, during which time negotiations continued between Henry, Thomas, and the papacy. The same Abbot Peter of Celle, who declined to offer Thomas spiritual direction as chancellor, now congratulated him for defending the church's freedom. In 1169, from exile, Thomas as head of the church in England, excommunicated two bishops and threatened the entire country with interdict, that is, the cessation of all religious services. There would be no access to the sacraments of the church.

Eventually a form of reconciliation between king and archbishop was agreed and Thomas returned in triumph to Canterbury, but well aware that he was putting himself in peril. He refused to change his judgment on the two excommunicated bishops and on his suspension of the Archbishop of York. Henry, known for his temper, flew into a rage in which he ended with the question, "Will no one rid me of this meddlesome priest?" Given Henry's habitual rages, it is most unlikely that he intended this as a license to murder Thomas. However, four of his knights understood it as precisely that, license to kill an archbishop. They murdered Thomas in Canterbury Cathedral on

December 29, 1170.[138] The sacrilege immediately created a hostile reaction throughout the Christian world. Thomas's burial place in the cathedral became the most popular place of pilgrimage after Rome, illustrated by the well-known *Canterbury Tales* of Geoffrey Chaucer, and also illustrated by the less well-known pilgrimage of Lothar Segni/Pope Innocent III.

Archbishop Baldwin of Ford

Baldwin was a native of Exeter. He became Archdeacon of Totnes, Devon, in 1161. Towards the end of 1169, he entered the Cistercian Abbey of Ford, and was elected abbot in 1175. It is from the Abbey of Ford that he takes the name by which he is most commonly known, Baldwin of Ford. The date of his entry into the Cistercians is hardly circumstantial. Less than one year later, on December 29, 1170, Thomas Becket was murdered. Baldwin had been a strong supporter of Thomas. He would have seen in Thomas a martyr's demonstration of his teacher Robert Pullen's political theology of the final superiority of the spiritual over the temporal. Undoubtedly, a combination of growing frustration with the destructive quarrel between king and church, the venality of the upper clergy, and an intense desire to live a more radically evangelical life led him to the Cistercians.

Beryl Smalley comments: "The Becket conflict may have influenced his decision to become a monk, but he certainly had a vocation."[139] Small wonder then that Baldwin's treatise on the Eucharist would have the character of "a call for spiritual reform, for a return to the Gospel text."[140] At a time when the church in England was riven with scandal, culminating in the murder of an archbishop in his cathedral, Baldwin sought to emphasize the Eucharist, *the* sacrament of communion, as the very heart of the Christian life. His treatise was dedicated to an older Exeter pupil of Robert Pullen, Bartholomew, now Bishop of Exeter.

Baldwin was appointed Bishop of Worcester in 1180, and in 1184 he was elected Archbishop of Canterbury, but this was to be problematic. The bishops of the province chose Baldwin as archbishop, but he was not the choice of the monks of Christ Church, Canterbury, who were opposed to Baldwin's Cistercian asceticism, and who had chosen the Abbot of Battle as archbishop.

Baldwin created a college of secular priests at Hakington, about a half-mile from Canterbury. To do this he diverted funds from the monastery of Christ Church, which was lavishly endowed. The monks appealed against their archbishop to Rome, and won their case. However, Baldwin had the king's support, the same King Henry in whose reign Becket had been murdered. Eventually, a compromise was reached in 1189, and Baldwin founded his college near Lambeth. Baldwin had learned that political theological theory, like the art of politics itself, is the art of the possible, and he learned to get along with Henry.

He accompanied Henry's son, Richard I (*Coeur de Lion*) on the third crusade. He became ill and died at Acre in 1190. It is said that "his grief at the lack of discipline of the Christian armies probably hastened his death."[141] He left his money for the liberation of the Holy Land.

Baldwin on the Eucharist

Baldwin composed one of the longest medieval treatises on the Eucharist, *On the Sacrament of the Altar*.[142] Yet, as David Bell, the foremost North American commentator on Baldwin has it, "the theological importance of this learned and austere archbishop has been strangely neglected."[143] He does not feature in many contemporary textbooks in eucharistic theology, and he remains an interest mainly for medieval specialists. However, arguably his theological reflections on the Eucharist have much to say to us today.

Before elucidating some aspects of Baldwin's eucharistic theology, let us first attend to the specific genre of his treatise. His theology is monastic, not scholastic, and so David Bell comments: "We may see in Baldwin one of the last true representations of a rich monastic theological tradition which was soon to be followed up in the inexorable advance of philosophical scholasticism."[144] The treatise is a work of liturgical theology as we might put it today. It is not controlled or determined by the analytic methodological presuppositions of scholastic theology.[145] He shows no interest in what might be described as the "mechanics" of the eucharistic theology. He is far more concerned with its immediate meaning for Christian life. Baldwin knew of such "mechanics," but it is the Eucharist as it makes the church, the Eucharist within the totality of the Christian mystery that both attracts him and compels him to write. He is utterly suspicious of what he takes to be arrogant intellectual explorations of this greatest of Christian mysteries.

At the center of the Eucharist is Christ's desire to unite himself more closely with all who are church. Faith in Christ is, therefore, necessary for fruitful participation in the sacrament. There is no automatic or magical flow of grace for Baldwin. Faith is fundamental. He distinguishes two levels of eating the Eucharist: sacramental eating and spiritual eating. Sacramental eating is for him physical presence at the celebration, physical eating. Sacramental eating at its most fruitful includes spiritual eating. It is the eating of Christ of those who have faith in Christ.

However, this spiritual eating is not confined for Baldwin only to those who are explicitly Christian. Spiritual eating includes also those spiritual people who lived long before the Incarnation.[146] He has in mind particularly the great spiritual heroes of the Old Testament. Baldwin relates the Last Supper to events recounted in the Old Testament. His insight is powerfully expressed by Dom Jean Leclercq: "What takes place on the altar is the summit, the resumé, the recapitulation of what had taken place on all the altars men have raised since their creation, of all that God has done for them and continues to do. The passage of time is only a divine pedagogical method by which humanity is taught progressively to take part in the Mass."[147] Though Baldwin does not explicitly develop his theology in this direction—it would be entirely anachronistic—this spiritual eating of the Eucharist echoes the positive strains of Christo-centrism presupposed in Karl Rahner's too-often-misunderstood theology of the anonymous Christian.

Dom Jean Leclercq has as the title of one of the sub-sections in his "Introduction" to *On the Sacrament of the Altar,* "Théologie Admirative." Favored words of Baldwin for the proper attitude to the Eucharist are *stupor* and *admiratio. Admiratio* means "wonder," or perhaps we might say "amazement." Baldwin espouses a theology of wonder or amazement at the gift of the Eucharist. "[Baldwin] never ceases to admire—to admire the mystery of revelation, to admire those who believe in the church; he admires the faith."[148]

Baldwin refuses to be polemical or controversial, with but one exception. He demonstrates a somewhat anti-Greek stance when he inveighs against their use of leavened bread in the Eucharist, the so-called azymite controversy. Baldwin in this context uses of the Greeks the verb *judaizare,* "to Judaize," implying a refusal or at least reluctance on the part of the Greeks to move, as he sees it, from the Old Testament to the New. His argument rests on the stock conviction of the times, supported by his own exegesis of the Gospel texts, that Christ at the Last Supper, a Passover meal, used unleavened bread. To take Christ at his word, therefore, the Greeks should use unleavened bread too. But, apart from this, there are no signs of controversial theology in Baldwin's treatment of the Eucharist.

Having learned it from his teacher, Robert Pullen, Baldwin uses the term "transubstantiation" to refer to the change from bread and wine to the body and blood of Christ. He is aware that the tradition has used a variety of terms for this change, for example, *transubstantiatur*, "is transubstantiated," *mutatur*, "is changed," *convertitur*, "is turned into." "Despite this diversity of terms," says Baldwin, "it is the same piety and confession of faith."[149] At the same time, he wishes to distance himself from any term that might suggest that the change is less than ontological. It is a real change.

His condemned contemporary, Berengar of Tours (ca. 1010–88), seems to have preferred the eucharistic change to be described as "figurative," the bread and wine remaining "substantially" what they were. Baldwin, but without acerbity or polemic, is singularly unhappy with the notion of the "transfiguration" of the bread and wine into the body and blood of Christ. "It is true, I say, that this change is not according to the figure, but according to the substance."[150] The bread is not transfigured—that is not a *real* enough term for and smacks of subjectivism—but is transubstantiated. *Figura* or transfiguration seems to Baldwin to admit of the possibility of deception so that the eucharistic change would not necessarily be a change *in natura*, "in nature."

He refers to St. Paul. In 2 Corinthians 11:14, we read: "Even Satan disguises himself as an angel of light" (NRSV). This disguise could be described as a "transfiguration." Satan is not *really* changed into an angel of light, but is "transfigured." This is deception. In the Eucharist there can be no deception, since it is not human action but God's action. God cannot deceive. To underscore the ontology of God's action, "transubstantiation" is preferred as a more adequate term for the eucharistic change. It is a more adequate term, even if it is something of a new term for Baldwin. He points out that "consubstantial" for the Word, and "persons" for the Trinity were in their own times new terms.[151] We ought not to be afraid of new theological language, but only of such language as would radically change the received meaning of the faith.

Even though Berengar may be in the background here, Baldwin never mentions him by name. Why not? Because he was not a polemicist theologically, and also—in David Bell's words—"because Baldwin was not really interested in discussing dialectical and scholastic problems. His concern . . . was not *how* the eucharistic mystery takes place, but what the mystery is and how it affects us."[152] Transubstantiation for Baldwin is belief *that,* the eucharistic belief of the Christian tradition from the very beginning, not speculation *how*.

"The Mass reproduces the Supper, and the Supper refers to the entire life of Christ, particularly his passion, which would follow on the morrow." Jean Leclercq, in his magisterial summary of Baldwin's eucharistic theology, points out that the idea of the sacrifice of Calvary as an expiation offered to the justice of God is not found in Baldwin. "On the contrary, the sacrifice of Christ is 'a work of love, produced by love.' The love of Christ is the very principle of his oblation."[153]

Paradoxically in some respects, Baldwin seems closer here to the theology of Peter Abelard than to his predecessor in the see of Canterbury, St. Anselm. The cross is the work of love, not of justice, not of a debt in justice being paid to God the Father. This view of the cross and, therefore, of the eucharistic sacrifice which represents it, has practical implications. The eucharistic sacrifice signifies and makes present the love of Christ for us: "One bread for God, who rejoices in the brotherly love with which we love each other and is, as it were, nourished by us. And we ourselves are also one bread for each other, for our mutual love is our mutual comfort and our mutual nourishment.... We are one body through charity, by which Christ is loved as the Spouse, who also loves the church as his own body."[154]

Pulling together Baldwin's challenging theology on the Eucharist as sacrifice, Leclercq writes: "Just as Jesus offered himself, we must offer ourselves, and just as he has given his life for us, we must give ours for our brothers. The proper effect of communion is the grace to give ourselves."[155] Baldwin's eucharistic theology has an exceptionally contemporary ring to it.

Baldwin discusses martyrdom in the *Sacrament of the Altar.* Beryl Smalley reminds us that the treatise was written "within ten years of Becket's death."[156] Although he does not mention Thomas by name, Baldwin clearly has him in mind: "Wine is changed into blood when righteousness rejoices, and it is decided to resist unrighteousness at the cost of bloodshed. That is righteousness perfected.... If a righteous man girds himself with the sword against trial or persecution, if he judges it better to die than to depart from righteousness, ... if he is found faithful in men's sight when he is brought to judgment for confession of faith or for defense of righteousness, then he shall be ranked with Christ in the judgment to come.... A man like this is worthy indeed to be called a martyr and appears as a faithful witness, giving his testimony in the land."[157] Beryl Smalley concludes: "The passage reads as a vindication of Thomas as a true martyr, with an implied reproach to his royal persecutor."[158] What Baldwin writes of Becket, and Smalley of Baldwin, could be said in our times of such martyrs as Archbishop Oscar

Romero, or indeed to those many Christians in parts of Nigeria or the Middle East who are being killed for their Christian faith.

Conclusion

Twelfth-century England was a very troubled period in the history of the church. The struggle between King Henry and St. Thomas Becket makes this abundantly clear, and especially the martyrdom of the latter. Nonetheless, it was also a very productive period for theology, and especially for eucharistic theology. Both Robert Pullen and Baldwin of Ford demonstrate this. Perhaps we need to delve more deeply and more regularly into the history of the church and the history of theology to gain true perspective on what we take to be the crises and troubles of our own time.

7

The Liturgical Margery Kempe

Richard Rolle was a visionary, Walter Hilton a Canon Regular and spiritual director, Julian of Norwich was an avowed anchoress: if these taught English spirituality, Margery received it and expressed it in the hurly-burly of Kings Lynn market place.

MARTIN THORNTON[159]

IF WE SKIP AHEAD from the twelfth century to the fourteenth and fifteenth centuries, and from the monastic and archiepiscopal Baldwin to the English lay-woman, Margery Kempe, we find ourselves in a quite different world in many respects, and yet Margery's eucharistic piety and devotion relates comfortably with Baldwin's theology. The opening words of Martin Thornton contrast the so very ordinary Margery Kempe with what we might call the "professional" religious—Richard Rolle, Walter Hilton, and Julian of Norwich. Whenever the name of Margery Kempe crops up in theology, it usually has to do with spirituality or the history of asceticism or perhaps mysticism, but never with the liturgy. In one sense, that is as it ought to be. She was not a theologian, let alone a liturgical theologian, nor is she a major source for the developing history of the liturgy. However, in another sense it seems unfortunate because as a late medieval married woman, not a nun nor a monk nor a friar, the mainstay of her spiritual life would undoubtedly have been the liturgy. She had direct access to nothing else. This chapter seeks to look at something of the liturgy through the experience of Margery Kempe.

Margery Kempe

"Nowhere in Christian literature is there a character quite like Margery Kempe, and nowhere is there a book of mystical devotion quite like hers."[160] Margery Kempe, born about 1373 in Bishop's Lynn, Norfolk (now known as King's Lynn), is one of the most ordinary yet striking figures of the late Middle Ages, and her narrated biography, *The Book of Margery Kempe*, offers rich insights into the religious life of the laity of her day. It is the first autobiography in the English language. Margery was illiterate, and her spiritual life story was dictated to her anonymous priest-amanuensis, in all likelihood Robert Spryngolde. Though we do not know the date of her death, it was after 1438, when she dictated her book and was admitted into the Guild of the Trinity in Bishop's Lynn.

The daughter of a burgess, John Brunham, she came of a prosperous family and was married to a merchant, John Kempe, when she was about twenty years old. Following the birth of her first child, Margery experienced what can only be described as a combination of spiritual crisis and the complete breakdown of her mental health. According to her own testimony, "She had a thing on her conscience which she had never revealed before that time in all her life."[161] We are not told the nature of her unconfessed sin, and scholarly guesses range from sexual sin (in the course of her story Margery reveals her temptation to sexual intercourse with a man other than her husband) to Lollardy, which was rife in her part of England at the time. It is noteworthy, for example, that William Sawtrey, the very first priest to be burned for Lollardy in 1401, served in Bishop's Lynn for some time prior to 1399.[162] Margery must have known Sawtrey, even though his name never appears in her book. It has been suggested that the omission is entirely deliberate—perhaps even a scribal caution—to distance her from the condemned Lollards.[163]

Following the birth of her first child, she thought she was going to die and sent for the priest to confess her sins, but she could not even then bring herself to confess this particular sin. The priest, Robert Spryngolde, dealt with her impatiently, and, accompanied with all the medieval pictures of hellfire and punishment especially for unconfessed sin, she had a complete nervous breakdown. Later, Margery was to say of her priest, whom she came to love, respect, and depend on: "I can never pay [Master Robert] back for his goodness to me, and the gracious trouble he has taken in hearing my confession."[164]

After receiving a vision of Christ, her health improved. This vision of Christ was very firmly fixed in her memory. Though it was written down some twenty years later, the vision remained very fresh: "Our Lord Jesus Christ . . . appeared to his creature who had forsaken him, in the likeness of a man, the most seemly, most beauteous, and most amiable that ever might be seen with man's eye, clad in a mantle of purple silk, sitting upon her bedside, looking upon her with so blessed a countenance that she was strengthened in all her spirits . . ."[165] When she recovered, however, Margery sank back into her former, worldly ways. She enjoyed fine and fashionable clothes and fine living, and she threw herself into a number of business ventures in the town, none of which were really successful. In twenty years of marriage she had thirteen further children, and yet we know nothing of them, not even their names.

Margery's true conversion came sometime later in an experience that was to alter her life: "One night, as this creature lay in bed with her husband, she heard a melodious sound so sweet and delectable that she thought she had been in Paradise. Immediately she jumped out of bed and said, 'Alas that I ever sinned! It is full merry in heaven.' This melody was so sweet that it surpassed all the melody that might be heard in this world, without any comparison, and it caused this creature when she afterwards heard any mirth or melody to shed very plentiful tears of high devotion, with great sobbings and sighings for the bliss of heaven, not fearing the shames and contempt of this wretched world."[166]

Probably in her late twenties, Margery had reached the point where she wished to give herself entirely to Christ. The year 1413 seems to have been the time when this desire reached its highest point of satisfaction. Marjorie was about forty years old, her father had just died, and she and John entered into an arrangement, a mutual vow of chastity that would enable her to live a more or less completely religious life-style. Some suggest that her father's death may have removed a "restraining influence" from Margery's life, and that both the death and the consequent legacy made it "psychologically as well as financially possible" for her to develop a more independent and comprehensive religious way of life.[167]

Margery was favored with the gift of tears and sobbed frequently, perhaps especially during the liturgy. She quoted Holy Scripture frequently and this, as we shall see, got her into trouble. She undertook arduous pilgrimages not only within England to well-established pilgrimage centers, but also abroad to the Holy Land, Assisi, Rome, Compostela, as well as to other places in Northern Europe after escorting her widowed daughter-in-law home to Gdansk. Margery's visions and heavenly locutions pepper her book, and ultimately one has to come to some judgment about them. I tend to side with the judgment of Dom David Knowles, who, though sympathetically portraying Margery, believes that many of her extraordinary "experiences" can be credited to "her very lively faculty of subconscious imagination."[168] Knowles's judgment, in the face of the evidence, is less harsh than that of Dom François Vandenbroucke: "Her excited tone awakens distrust and makes the reader wonder whether she is not a case for a psychiatrist rather than a theologian."[169] As Margery moves through her world, she offers us descriptions of her liturgical/sacramental experience, and it is to these that we shall now attend, beginning with the Scriptures.

The Holy Scriptures

Margery quotes the Holy Scriptures throughout her book. Since she was unable to read, her knowledge came from remembering passages that had been read to her, from sermons, from discussions with her confessors. Her memory must have been remarkable because at will she can recall passages that fit the various circumstances in which she finds herself.

Her practice of quoting Scripture got her into difficulties with the ecclesiastical authorities of the time. She was charged with Lollardy—the Lollards were much given to citing Scripture—and was brought before church courts in Leicester, York, and Beverly. In Beverly people shouted at her, not only expressing their frustration with her religiosity but also with her lack of convention: "Woman, give up this life that you lead, and go and spin, and card wool, as other women do, and do not suffer so much shame and so much unhappiness."[170] Women were not expected to be conversant with scriptural and theological matters. It was not just the ordinary townsfolk of Beverly who felt this way. Once Margery approached Richard Caister, the parish priest of St. Stephen's Church, Norwich, seeking to speak with him and to learn from him. "She greeted the Vicar, asking him if she could—in the afternoon, when he had eaten—speak with him for an hour or two of the love of God. He, lifting up his hands and blessing himself, said 'Bless us! How could a woman occupy one or two hours with the love of our Lord? I shan't eat a thing until I find out what you can say of our Lord God in the space of an hour.'"[171] As it happened, Caister was won over by Margery and became one of her defenders.

On an occasion in which she was in Canterbury, Margery found herself in conversation about Scripture to some monks. A young monk said to her, "Either you have the Holy Ghost or else you have a devil within you, for what you are speaking here to us is Holy Writ, and that you do not have of yourself." Ability to quote Scripture with ease and to do so with regularity was an almost sure sign of affiliation with the Lollards. So, as she left this monastic community after speaking with them, they followed her and cried out: "'You shall be burned, you false Lollard! Here is a cartful of thorns ready for you, and a barrel to burn you with!' And the creature stood outside the gates of Canterbury—for it was in the evening—with many people wondering at her. Then people said, 'Take her and burn her!'"[172] The incident provides some understanding of how conversant with Scripture Margery was, and the very real dangers that this brought about. The late Anglican pastoral theologian, Martin Thornton, probably has it right when he says of Margery: "She was a bit of a 'preacher' and doubtless something of a feminist as well, which was no more popular in ecclesiastical circles in the fifteenth century than it was in the nineteenth!"[173]

The Eucharist

An anonymous Benedictine nun of Stanbrook Abbey wrote of Margery's eucharistic faith earlier last century, not long after *The Book of Margery Kempe* was first published: "[Margery's] book shows clearly enough the reverence and devotion of fifteenth-century England towards the Blessed Sacrament."[174] The author states immediately that Margery's eucharistic thinking is entirely orthodox and that she cannot be thought of as a kind of harbinger of the Reformation like John Wyclif.

However, one area in which she remains quite distinct from the normal sacramental practice of the time is the frequency with which she received Holy Communion. Margery believed herself to have received direct instructions from the Lord to receive weekly communion. Christ said to her: "Instead of meat you shall eat my flesh and my blood, that is the true body of Christ in the sacrament of the altar. This is my will, daughter, that you receive my body every Sunday, and I shall cause so much grace to flow into you that everyone shall marvel at it."[175] The year 1413, the year that initiated her great pilgrimages, Margery sought an audience with the Archbishop of Canterbury, Thomas Arundel, seeking his permission for her to receive regular communion. "When she came into his presence she made her obeisances to him as best she could, praying him, out of his gracious lordship, to grant her authority to choose her confessor and to receive communion every Sunday . . . under his letter and his seal throughout all his province. And he granted her with great kindness her whole desire without any silver or gold, nor would he let his clerks take anything for the writing or sealing of the letter."[176] Similarly, in 1417, she sought a similar letter of authority from Arundel's successor, Henry Chichele, giving her permission to choose her confessor as well as to receive communion every week.[177] This would have been quite extraordinary at the time. For example, Lady Margaret Beaufort (1443–1509), the grandmother of King Henry VIII, received communion but once a month and she was considered "something of a prodigy."[178]

Margery had special eucharistic experiences, probably to be interpreted along the lines suggested by David Knowles—"her lively faculty of subconscious imagination"—from which we may select the following:

> One day this creature was hearing Mass, a young man and a good priest was holding up the sacrament in his hands over his head, and the sacrament shook and fluttered to and fro just as a dove flutters her wings. And when he held up the chalice with the precious sacrament, the chalice moved to and fro as if it would have fallen out of his hands. When the consecration was done, this creature marveled at the stirring and moving of the Blessed Sacrament, wanting to see more consecrations and looking to see if it would do it again. Then our Lord Jesus Christ said to the creature, "You will not see it any more in this way; therefore, thank God that you have seen it. My daughter Bridget never saw me in this way."[179]

The Bridget referred to is St. Bridget of Sweden, to whom Margery was especially devoted. In a time given to eucharistic miracles, there is nothing remarkable here, but what is interesting is that this particular experience was not to be repeated. The failure of repetition of the experience may not simply mean that Margery had been greatly favored and would not be so again. It may also be that Margery has not only "a lively faculty of subconscious imagination," but perhaps is "subconsciously" aware of it! Perhaps she knows that in the intensity of her devotion at Mass, she can be carried away.

In 1417 Margery went on trial for suspected Lollardy in Leicester, a well-known center of the heresy. John Wyclif, the Oxford theologian, had denied transubstantiation, and so his Lollard followers were constantly questioned about the Eucharist. Brought before the abbot of St. Mary's Abbey, Leicester, Margery was questioned about her eucharistic beliefs. She made this reply: "Sirs, I believe in the sacrament of the altar in this way: that whatever man has taken the order of priesthood, be he ever so wicked a man in his manner of life, if he duly say those words over the bread that our Lord Jesus Christ said when he celebrated the Last Supper sitting among his disciples, I believe that it is his very flesh and his blood, and no material bread; nor may it ever be unsaid, be it once said."[180] This response of Margery shows that she accepts the doctrine of transubstantiation, and removes her from the suspicion of being a follower of Wyclif.[181]

The gift of tears was much appreciated in the Middle Ages, exemplified in such visionaries as Francis of Assisi, Angela of Foligno, and Bridget of Sweden.[182] Margery prays to receive communion with tears. "Lord, as surely as you are not angry with me, grant me a well of tears, through which I may receive your precious body with all manners of tears of devotion to your worship and the increasing of merit; for you are my joy, Lord, my bliss, my comfort, and all the treasure that I have in this world . . ."[183]

It appears that the reserved sacrament was brought in procession to situations of possible public calamity. Margery tells us of a great fire in Lynn in 1421, a fire that burned down the Guildhall, and threatened the parish church of St. Margaret. After the priest sought Margery's advice, this is what took place: "Her confessor, parish priest of St. Margaret's Church, took the precious sacrament and went before the fire as devoutly as he could and afterwards brought it back to into the church again—and the sparks of fire flew about the church." Margery follows in this procession, weeps and prays much, and later is brought the news by "three worthy men": "Look, Margery, God has shown us great grace and sent us a fair snowstorm to quench the fire with. Be now of good cheer, and thank God for it."[184]

The Liturgical Year

Margery adds little to what we know of medieval liturgical ceremonies through the Christian year, but the details she offers make these ceremonies quite graphic.[185] Late medieval Christians were encouraged mentally to imagine the events celebrated in the liturgy, almost as "the ideal way of participating in the church's worship."[186] This was certainly Margery's experience. At Candlemas, "when the said creature saw people with their candles in church, her mind was ravished into beholding our Lady offering her beloved Son, our Saviour, to the priest Simeon in the Temple, as veritably to her spiritual understanding as if she had been there in her bodily presence to offer with our Lady herself." She tells us of "the heavenly songs that she thought she heard when our blissful Lord was offered up to Simeon." Margery so enters imaginatively into the events of Candlemas that "she could scarcely carry up her own candle to the priest, as people did at the time of the offering, but went on reeling about on all sides . . ."[187] The liturgical year was celebrated to bring about intense feelings, a strong sense of participation, on the part of the laity. But it was not just Margery's powerful imaginative entering into the events that brought about the effects described. There was also the objective given, of the liturgy, its music, gestures, and structure, varying according to the liturgical season. Eamon Duffy, for example, believes that "the heavenly songs" Margery heard were in fact heavenly songs, that is to say, the splendid liturgical chants of the day that easily came within the resources of an urban church like St. Margaret's, Lynn.[188]

On Palm Sunday there was a special ceremony involving the reserved Eucharist. Having been placed in a shrine or tent in the churchyard, it was brought forth to meet the palm procession coming out of the church. The procession knelt before the sacrament, kissing the ground, and then all went on to the churchyard cross. There the Passion of the Lord was sung. The shrine with the sacrament was then held above the church doorway, so that all entering the church had to pass under it. She describes a strange ritual gesture. "On the same Sunday, the priest took the staff of the cross and smote on the church door, the door was opened to him; and then the priest entered with the sacrament . . ."[189] This gesture was apparently forbidden by the rubricists, but it was popular with the people, and was intended to symbolize, through demanding entry into the church, Christ's harrowing of hell, after coming forth from death.[190] Margery describes the entire liturgical events of Palm Sunday "as if she had been in Jerusalem," and then adds that she wept copiously during the celebration of the Mass.

At Easter 1433, while accompanying her daughter-in-law home to Gdansk, her ship put in at a Norwegian port. On Easter Sunday the master, crew, and most of the passengers went to the services in the local church. This included the service of raising the cross "from the tomb." Then she tells us that on Easter Monday, the sacrament was brought on board and all received communion.[191]

On the Feast of Corpus Christi, there was the ever popular procession, and this too evokes tears from Margery: "When she saw the precious sacrament borne about the town with lights and reverence, the people kneeling on their knees, then she had many holy thoughts and meditations, and then she would often cry out and roar, as though she would have burst, for the faith and the trust that she had in the precious sacrament."[192]

The Gift of Tears

"The gift of tears" is not something liturgical. Since, however, it often accompanies Margery during liturgical celebrations, it deserves some comment. Her life was made particularly difficult by this gift of loud and frequent tears. That she has questions about this gift emerges from her visit to the famed anchoress, Dame Julian of Norwich. Julian told her: "When God visits a soul with tears of contrition, devotion or compassion, he may and ought to believe that the Holy Ghost is in his soul. . . . No evil spirit may give these tokens . . ."[193] Though somewhat reassured by Julian, Margery continued to be troubled by this gift throughout her life. Both Margery's parish priest, Robert Spryngolde, and her spiritual counselor, the Carmelite Allan of Lynn, believed that this was a true gift of the Holy Spirit. They believed that the tears came only when God willed them, and that she was not in a position of control over them. We get a sense of the complex meaning of and reaction to the tears from this passage in chapter 28:

> God would visit her with [tears], sometimes in church, sometimes in the street, sometimes in her chamber, sometimes in the fields, when God would send them, for she never knew the time nor hour when they would come. And they never came without surpassingly great sweetness of devotion and high contemplation. And as soon as she perceived that she was going to cry, she would hold it in as much as she could, so that people would not hear it and get annoyed. For some said it was a wicked spirit tormented her; some said it was an illness; some said she had drunk too much wine; some cursed her; some wished she was on the sea in a bottomless boat; and so each man as he thought. Other, spiritually inclined men loved her and esteemed her all the more.[194]

Though Margery's weeping brought about different reactions, it was certainly not in intent a self-centered expression of spirituality. Margery tells us that she wept when she encountered the sick being anointed, or when people were dying.[195] Her tears in this respect were her expression of John Donne's famous aphorism that "No man is an island, entire of itself." Where Donne and so many in the Christian community superbly craft words to bring to expression this theologically rooted notion of persons-in-relation,

Margery weeps. Historian Clarissa Atkinson has it right when she describes Margery's tears; "She *was called to weep and to pray for the souls of her fellow Christians,* and to do so not in a cell or a convent, but in the world."[196] The tears were an expression of a deep spirituality of communion. Margery knew that "one person is no person," that all Christians are knit together in the Body of Christ, and her tears were shed on behalf of all. Historical theologian, Ellen Ross, considers Margery as both "representative of humanity to God," and "representative of God to humanity." She reminds her peers of the God of mercy while, through her tears, she asks for God's mercy for them "for whom she is God's minister."[197]

Though many found her weeping during the celebration of the liturgy disturbing—she frequently tells us so—medieval worshipers were familiar with disturbances. Margaret Gallyon summarily describes what must have been fairly commonplace: "Vergers fought a losing battle among noisy parishioners, who wandered in and out of church at will. Parish registers repeatedly record instances of rowdy behavior, chattering, laughing, joking, 'jangling and japing,' the playing of chess and gambling with dice during service and at sermon time."[198] Tears and noisy tears may have been a distraction, but probably not too much of one.

Margery's sense of communion with God, strengthened by all her spiritual practices, both liturgical/sacramental and others, has built up in her a pervasive christocentrism, "a kind of extra life concurrent with her own and which she sees suffused, super-imposed, simultaneous, with the world of ordinary streets and rooms, humble mothers and their children."[199] A commonplace example of her christocentrism arises from the experience of cooking stockfish (mainly cod, codling, and haddock). Stockfish were cured by being opened and dried in the sun. When the fish was boiled, the skin would often stick to one's hands, and this quotidian example affords Margery insight of communion with Christ. She hears the Lord speaking to her: "Daughter, you are obedient to my will, and cleave as fast to me as the skin of the stockfish sticks to man's hand when it is boiled, and you will not forsake me for any shame that any man may do to you."[200]

Conclusion

Arguably, the liturgy in all its manifestations but focused on the Eucharist, was the center of Margery Kempe's spirituality. As a laywoman, she had no direct access to the extra-liturgical apparatus of monastic communities.

From the liturgy, including preaching, she absorbs all she needs to progress in the life of holiness. And more. Margery stands as an excellent example of what Vatican II's "Constitution on the Church" chapter 5, calls "the universal call to holiness. "It is well put by Margaret Gallyon: "By her life of prayer and religious devotion she utterly refutes the notion that religion and mystical encounter with the Divine Being are for clergy and cloistered celibates only. Her approach to God is through Christ, and Christ, she believes, is for all people everywhere at all time."[201]

8

The Eucharistic Richard Hooker (1554–1600)

Hooker was discriminating in his view of the Continental Reformers. He is hostile to extreme Calvinism and, in his emphasis on reason, moral discipline, and sacramental grace, he has more in common with the Caroline Divines of the following century.

PAUL AVIS[202]

THE ECUMENICAL MOVEMENT OF the twentieth century has brought Christians together in ways undreamed of, since the East-West split of the eleventh century and the Reformations of the sixteenth century. It is important that Christians live with a passion for church unity. Instead of learning our faith and articulating our theology against other Christians, it is necessary that we learn and articulate with other Christians, that we develop the habit of seizing on what is common long before we move to what may be different in our retrieval of the great Christian tradition. Part of that passion, at least for those with an interest in theology or a responsibility for teaching theology, must involve reading the theological texts of other ecclesial traditions. This essay is a brief engagement with the theological work, especially the eucharistic teaching of the sixteenth-century Anglican priest-theologian, Richard Hooker.

The Elizabethan Settlement

"Richard Hooker, the true father of Anglicanism much more than Cranmer or Henry VIII, was a humble country parson, but vastly erudite." Thus, Louis Bouyer on Richard Hooker.[203] What might be described as essential Anglicanism owes much to what was achieved during the reign of Queen Elizabeth I, daughter of Henry VIII and Anne Boleyn. The Queen was interested in theological matters. Thus, she read her New Testament in Greek regularly, her private book of devotions was full of prayers for "Thy Church my care," she saw to the elimination of the so-called Black Rubric forbidding kneeling at Holy Communion—from the Book of Common Prayer, and believed in the eucharistic presence of Christ. She was a strong supporter of episcopacy though her own preference was also for a celibate clergy and episcopate, and she consistently refused to receive at court the wives of her married bishops, nor did she allow the wives of clergy to live in colleges or in cathedral closes. At a time when the Puritans were vociferously denouncing episcopacy as a Romish creation far from the New Testament, Elizabeth described their position as "newfangledness." As she said once to the Spanish ambassador de Silva, "We only differ from other Catholics in things of small importance."[204]

When Richard Hooker was about eleven years old in 1565, Bishop Grindal of London described the liturgical condition of his diocese in terms that have a remarkably contemporary sound:

> Some say the service and the prayers in the chancel, others in the body of the church; some say the same in a seat made in the church, some in the pulpit with their faces to the people; some keep precisely to the order of the book, others intermeddle psalms in metre; some say in a surplice, others without a surplice; the Table standeth in the body of the church in some places, in others it standeth in the chancel; in some places the Table standeth altarwise, distant from the wall a yard, in some others in the middle of the chancel, north and south; in some places the Table is joined, in others it standeth upon trestles; in some places the Table hath a carpet, in others it hath not; administration of the Communion is done by some with surplice and cap, some with surplice alone, others with none; some with chalice, some with a communion cup, others with a common cup; some with unleavened bread, some with leavened; some receive kneeling, others standing, others sitting.[205]

Elizabeth may have demanded publicly and hoped privately for uniformity of liturgical practice, but then as now such uniformity is impossible to achieve even as its desirability is in some measure debatable.

Richard Hooker

Richard Hooker was born in 1554 at Heavitree in Exeter, in the southwest of England. His early education took place at Exeter Grammar School, and his uncle, John Hooker, was the school-master. The schoolmaster was on friendly terms with the Bishop of Salisbury, John Jewel, and the latter saw to it that the younger Hooker had a place at Oxford University. He entered Corpus Christi College, Oxford, where he became a Fellow of the College and Deputy Professor of Hebrew when the regular professor, Thomas Kingsmill, was prevented by illness from teaching.

Ordained a priest in the Church of England probably about 1581, Hooker remained in academic life at Oxford until his arrival in London in 1585. In that year he was appointed Master of the Temple by the Archbishop of Canterbury, John Whitgift. This was an important appointment. The Temple Church was at the Inns of Court, the very heart of the legal system, and the Master was the principal clergyman. It was here that Hooker began to develop his theology against the attacks of the Puritan divine, Walter Travers, a radical Calvinist who viewed the episcopal ordination of the Church of England as contrary to the New Testament. As one commentator has it, "It was the grit of Puritanism that brought out of the oyster the pearl which consists of the theological writings of Richard Hooker."[206] It was here that he laid the systematic groundwork of the Elizabethan Settlement of Religion.

Louis Bouyer compares Hooker's great work *The Laws of Ecclesiastical Polity*, begun at the Temple, with St. Thomas Aquinas's *Summa Theologiae*, although Bouyer would see Hooker more as a moralist and Aquinas more as a metaphysician.[207] *The Laws of Ecclesiastical Polity* is his basic response to the fundamental tenets of Puritanism. The first four books of the *Laws* were published in 1593, aided by his former pupil Edwin Sandys. In 1595 Hooker moved to the parish of Bishopsbourne near Canterbury. It was at Bishopsbourne that he published Book V of the *Laws* in 1597. Izaak Walton describes Hooker's death at forty-six years of age: "'Are my books and written papers safe? Then it matters not; for no other loss can trouble me' . . . and then the doctor (his confessor, Saravia) gave him and some of those friends which were with him, the blessed Sacrament of the body and blood of our Jesus."[208] When he died in 1600, three further books were readied for posthumous publication in 1648 and 1662. How is Hooker's theological style to be described?

The Theologian

Hooker's theology gets labeled in different ways by different scholars, and yet it has a universal appeal. Let us turn to three interpreters of Hooker to get an overall sense of his theology. The Irish Anglican, Archbishop Henry McAdoo, offers the following description of Hooker and it seems right on the mark: "If 'liberal' means 'an openness in the search for truth' rather than an accommodating and over-hospitable mind; if a 'conservative' is one who respects continuity, treasuring tradition's best and most durable gifts from the past, rather than being neurotically resistant to change, then, with some caution, one might say . . . that Hooker is a liberal conservative."[209] Here then is a theologian not easily pigeonholed, not easily put into a specific category. The distinguished Hooker scholar of over thirty years, John Booty, describes his subject in these fine words: "Through the years the conviction has grown in me that here is a man who understood."[210] "Here is a man who understood" suggests suasively a "liberal conservative," for the terms "liberal" and "conservative" on their own in theology are seldom accurate and dialogically barren. Finally, the popular apologist, C. S. Lewis, could write of Hooker: "Every system offers us a model of the universe; Hooker's model has unsurpassed grace and majesty. . . . Few model universes are more filled—one might say, more drenched—with Deity than his."[211] To say that someone's model of the universe is drenched with God is perhaps the ultimate accolade for a Christian.

For Hooker there are three ways of knowing: through our senses, through reason, and through what he calls "prophetical revelation" or Holy Scripture.[212] Knowing through Scripture is superior, but it may not stand on its own apart from reason. Scripture itself presupposes reason—how else could we know Scripture *as* Scripture—and the God of Scripture gifts us with reason in order the better to know him as he draws humankind to communion with himself. In this fashion he opposes any view of *sola Scriptura*.

He certainly had a strong reverence for tradition: "Neither may we in this case lightly esteem what hath been allowed as fit in the judgment of antiquity, and by the long continued practice of the whole Church; from which unnecessarily to swerve, experience hath never as yet found it safe."[213] There can be for him no jettisoning of tradition coming from antiquity that has served the church well. At the same time, that which comes from tradition cannot be reverenced and clung onto for its own sake: "Lest therefore the name of tradition should be offensive to any, considering how far by some it hath been and is abused, we mean by traditions, ordinances made in the prime of Christian religion, established with that authority which Christ hath left to his Church for matters indifferent, and in that consideration requisite to be observed, till like authority see just and reasonable cause to alter them."[214]

Hooker is referring to things that can be changed, that is to say matters of order, but never of doctrine. "The Church hath authority to establish that for an order at one time, which at another time it may abolish, and in both it may do well. But that which in doctrine the Church doth now deliver rightly as a truth, no man will say that it may hereafter recall, and as rightly avouch the contrary. Laws touching matter of order are changeable, by the power of the Church; articles concerning doctrine not so."[215] That which enables the alteration of tradition is the right exercise of human reason. Reason in that sense interprets Scripture. It is "an instrument which God doth use unto such purposes."[216] Hooker, therefore, accepts Holy Scripture as foundational, cherishes tradition, but sees reason as God's gift at work in both.

Ecclesiastical Polity 5

Book 5 of Hooker's *Laws of Ecclesiastical Polity* is the longest section in the collected work and has been described as "probably the first in-depth theological commentary on the Book of Common Prayer."[217] It is here that one finds his treatment of ecclesiology and of liturgical and sacramental issues, especially as he attends to Puritan objections. Booty writes of Hooker in terms that have a very contemporary ring: "He understood the Church as communion and community and that which makes it what it is meant to be: Word and sacraments administered by deacons, priests, and bishops in service to God and God's people."[218] Some citations will provide a sense of his ecclesiology. "Christ is whole with the whole Church and whole with every part of the Church, as touching his Person . . . It pleaseth him in mercy to account himself incomplete and maimed without us."[219] This is classical Pauline and patristic ecclesiology, but the phrase "maimed without us" is very interesting. "Maimed" means something like crippled or disfigured or mutilated. Hooker seems to suggest in these words that Christ cannot be Christ without us. That takes Augustine's *totus Christus* a stage further. His ecclesiology is never Gnostic, never an invisible church, but a church founded in the very crucified flesh of Christ: "Yea, by grace we are every one of us in Christ and in his Church, as by nature we are in those our first parents . . . and his Church he frameth out of the very flesh, the very wounded and bleeding side of the Son of Man."[220]

This very realist and high ecclesiology is not possible apart from the sacraments for Hooker. "This is, therefore, the necessity of sacraments. That saving grace which Christ originally is or hath for the general good of his whole Church, by sacraments he severally deriveth into every member thereof. . . . [Sacraments are] not physical but moral instruments of salvation," nor "bare resemblances or memorials of things absent, neither for naked signs and testimonies assuring us of grace received before but [as they are indeed and in verity] for means effectual . . . of . . . that grace available unto eternal life."[221] In this passage may be heard the debates about the meaning of the sacraments between Catholics and Reformed. Against the Reformed tradition, Hooker insists that the sacraments are not to be understood as "naked signs" assuring us of salvation, but must be seen as "effectual" means of grace. Against the Catholics, he is unhappy with the idea that the sacraments are physically instruments of salvation. Physics has to do with what may be sensibly approached—water, oil, bread, wine, laying on of hands. The sacraments, therefore, must be morally instruments of salvation, to do with the intellect and the will in the transformation of persons. Fundamentally, the sacraments have to do with participation, with grace, with deification in Christ through the Spirit. "Participation is that mutual inward hold which Christ hath of us and we of him."[222] "Participation" is a word he uses frequently for what the sacraments bring about. Christ binds us to himself through the sacraments and becomes the ground of our binding unto him. "Participation," or "deification," or "union with Christ" is a leitmotif of Hooker's theology:

> No good is infinite, but only God: therefore, he is our felicity and bliss. Moreover desire leadeth unto union with what it desireth. If then in him we are blessed, it is by force of participation and conjunction with him. Again it is not possession of any good thing that can make them happy which have it, unless they enjoy the thing wherewith they are possessed. Then are we happy therefore when fully we enjoy God, even as an object wherein the powers of our soul are satisfied, even with everlasting delight; so that although we be men, yet being unto God united we live as it were the life of God.[223]

This is the Athanasian *dictum* in Elizabethan language, "God became human that humans might be made divine." Hooker recognized with the entirety of the patristic tradition that the incarnation was not purely about Jesus *qua* Jesus, but also is "the ground for a renewing the entire human race."[224] It is not accidental that before he comes to the church and the sacraments he deals with christological and soteriological matters. His is a truly incarnational approach to theology. He placed "his whole sacramental analysis within an incarnational and soteriological framework."[225] If Christ is not *Deus,* his action in and through the sacraments could never *deify.*

This deifying mutual inward hold is clearly true of the Eucharist, but it is true not only of the Eucharist. "The grace which we have by the holy Eucharist doth not begin but continue life." The grace of Christ comes first through baptism, and this is the real life of the real God: "Our life begun in Christ is Christ . . ." But we need to grow, maintains Hooker, and graceful growth for him is not possible without the Eucharist. "Such as will live the life of God must eat the flesh and drink the blood of the Son of man, because this is a part of that diet which if we want we cannot live."[226]

There are tensions in Hooker's eucharistic theology in chapters 67 and 68 of Book 5 of *Ecclesiastical Polity,* especially with regard to the eucharistic presence of Christ and in respect of eucharistic sacrifice. Hooker is silent about sacrifice. This is what Bishop Kenneth Stevenson has to say on the point: "He is content to contemplate the sacrifice of Christ, and to see Christ's presence in the Eucharist in terms that border on the sacrificial. . . . But when in a later chapter he discusses priesthood, he passes over in a somewhat embarrassed manner the fact that the Early Fathers themselves used sacrificial language of the Eucharist."[227] In all variants of the Reformation tradition at this time, sacrifice was something of a neuralgic term when applied to the Eucharist. It trailed clouds of Catholicism, and of unsolved doctrinal issues. Hooker did not wish to be embroiled in this problematic. In fact, he seems to want to affirm somewhat variant eucharistic perspectives at the same time. It is clear, in line with his entire *oeuvre,* that he wants to distance himself from the Puritans. "It greatly offendeth, that some, when they labour to show the use of the holy Sacraments, assign unto them no end but only to teach the mind, by other senses, that which the Word doth teach by hearing."[228] In similar fashion, the Eucharist may not be understood simply as a sort of visual aid, a pedagogical help to the message of the Scriptures and preaching, a Puritan emphasis. The Eucharist is "not a shadow, destitute, empty and void of Christ."[229] Yet, Hooker can go on to say the following: "The real participation of Christ's body and blood is not therefore to be sought for in the sacrament, but in the worthy receiver of the sacrament."[230] This is perilously close to a receptionist view of the sacrament.

But, if one thinks of him now as a receptionist, what is one to make of this passage?

> Christ assisting this heavenly banquet with his personal and true presence doth by his own divine power add to the natural substance thereof supernatural efficacy, which addition to the nature of those consecrated elements changeth them and maketh them that unto us which otherwise they could not be; that to us they are thereby made such instruments as mystically yet truly, invisibly yet really work our communion or fellowship with the person of Jesus Christ as well as in that he is man as God, our participation also in the fruit, grace and efficacy of his body and blood, whereupon there ensueth a kind of transubstantiation in us, a true change both of soul and body, an alteration from death to life.[231]

Perhaps we might paraphrase Hooker here to the effect that the transubstantiation in us, which is the *telos* of the Eucharist, necessarily depends on the transubstantiation of the eucharistic elements, even if that term is not used. This is a near rendition, if not an actual rendition of traditional Catholic eucharistic theology. Indeed, John Booty does not hesitate to say that "Hooker nevertheless taught essentially the *Catholic* doctrine of the Eucharist."[232]

The question emerges, "What are we to make of these eucharistic tensions in Hooker?" The question admits of no easy answer. If one views the tensions from a position of iron-clad logic, then one might agree, in the words of the Anglican liturgical theologian Bishop Kenneth Stevenson, that "It is as if Hooker were (if the image is not appropriate here) trying to have his eucharistic cake and eat it."[233] Might there be another way of responding to these tensions? Might Hooker be offering an ecumenical eucharistic perspective, an eirenic perspective, a perspective that acknowledges the basic integrity of the Catholic tradition while simultaneously acknowledging the Reformation? Hooker is clearly aware of the Reformation-era debates about the eucharistic presence of Christ. He knows of the Puritans who eschew any traditional view of eucharistic presence, of the Lutherans who *consubstantiate* and of the Catholics who *transubstantiate*.[234] Hooker prefers meditation with silence on the Eucharist to verbal disputation. "I wish that men would more give themselves to meditate with silence what we have by the sacrament, and less to dispute the manner how."[235] He wants no part of "curious and intricate speculations": "[The Apostles] had at that time a sea of comfort and joy to wade in, and we by that which they did are taught that this heavenly food is given for the satisfying of our empty souls, and not for the exercising of our curious and subtle wits."[236] The contemporary Anglican theologian, George Pattison comments on this passage: "As Hooker saw only too clearly in his own time, and as the following century of religious wars more than demonstrated, such 'exercising of our curious and subtle wits' can only too quickly bring us back into a cycle of destruction in which angry words turn to angry blows and theoretical disputes prepare the way of terror and counter-terror by insurgencies and states alike."[237]

Conclusion

Having been companioned by Richard Hooker for three decades and more, the Anglican historian-theologian John Booty can say beautifully: "In an age of ever-increasing change, of being required to make decisions on the run, we need, from time to time, to be still, to reflect, to gain perspective, to cease our incessant chatter and to listen—to the wind, to the crying child, to music, to the beating of our hearts, and to the wisdom that comes through the occasionally difficult but carefully crafted words and phrases of a Richard Hooker."[238]

Booty is describing Hooker's overall theological achievement. But his words may just as easily be applied to our contemporary ecumenical situation. Being still, reflecting, ceasing our incessant chatter, and listening carefully to the theological sentiments of those in ecclesial traditions other than our own may lead to real discovery. Hooker may lead Catholics and Reformed to a deeper appreciation of the liturgical traditions of Anglicanism, and Anglicans to a deeper sense of identity in a rapidly changing ecclesial world.

9

Bishop Lancelot Andrewes (1555–1626), Liturgist

*Lancelot Andrewes . . . compares the church to a fire burning in the fireplace.
Baptizing a new Christian is like putting a new log on the fire; only gradually
does it catch fire and burn. The Christian life, then, becomes a process by which
individuals learn to make the church's faith their own.*

ROWAN A. GREER[239]

NOT TOO MANY CONTEMPORARY liturgists will have come across the Anglican theologian and bishop, Lancelot Andrewes (1555–1626), either in
their study of liturgy or in their prayer lives, and yet he is important in both
areas.[240] He certainly made a substantive contribution to the developing
liturgical theology of the Church of England and his prayers have continued to assist many in the spiritual life. One thinks for example, of John
Henry Newman who regularly prayed Andrewes's *Preces Privatae,* "private
prayers" prepared for his own personal use and unpublished until 1648.
Newman kept these prayers on his *pre-dieu* in the Birmingham Oratory
throughout his life there, and used them to make his thanksgiving after
Mass. As an Anglican Newman would naturally have had much in common with the high-church Andrewes. The same prayers, however, nurtured
the prayer-life of the ecumenical theologian and leader, originally Presbyterian, Lesslie Newbigin, who was to become a bishop in the united Church
of South India.[241] Small wonder then that Louis Bouyer speaks of Lancelot
Andrewes in such glowing terms: "Stupefyingly erudite, but even more
cultivated than erudite, he was none the less a pastor unreservedly devoted

to his flock, and, to cap all, practised a spirituality of inner contemplation that approached mysticism." Bouyer stops short at calling Andrewes a mystic, but there seems no good reason for that unless one entertains a highly specific model of mysticism. Andrewes is probably best understood as a liturgical mystic, that is to say, one whose awareness of and response to God are saturated, molded, and shaped by the liturgical tradition of the church that one can no longer differentiate the dynamic of the liturgy from the dynamic of life. Richard Hooker (1554–1600) in our previous chapter is generally regarded as the first major theologian to articulate the Anglican way in theology with due attention to Scripture, tradition, and reason. However, maintains Bouyer, "Andrewes may be viewed as the first pastor who tried with some success to get it adopted by the English Church mainly because he lived it with such rare intensity."[242] That intensity was thoroughly informed by his love and appreciation of the liturgy.

The works of Andrewes were collected and edited in the mid-nineteenth century by J. P. Wilson and J. Bliss as *The Works of Lancelot Andrewes,* 11 volumes (London: Parker, 1841–54). These volumes are inaccessible for most interested parties, and so in this chapter, use has been made of Andrewes's work as it has appeared in various anthologies and expositions of Anglican theology.

Lancelot Andrewes: Life and Context

Lancelot Andrewes was born in the parish of All Hallows, Barking, London in 1555 during the reign of Queen Mary. He was educated at Merchant Taylors' School and subsequently at Pembroke College, the University of Cambridge. During his high school years at Merchant Taylors', the principal was Richard Mulcaster, an Orientalist, and so Hebrew was taught in the school.[243] It was here that Andrewes developed his love for this language. At the time, Cambridge was the major center for Reformation teaching and so during his Cambridge years, he met many of "the rising tide of Puritans," but he himself was more interested in "the older traditions of Christian thought."[244] These older traditions are best summarized in Andrewes's own words; "One canon . . . two testaments, three creeds, four general councils, five centuries and the series of the Fathers in that period . . . determine the boundary of our faith."[245] The patristic period and theologies are central. Andrewes's aversion to Genevan Calvinism seems to be a parallel to his dislike for Roman scholasticism, both refusing a proper apophatism as he saw it, a proper silent and receptive reverence before the Mystery of God: "Andrewes always held that Calvinism tried to erect into a system what was essentially a mystery and thus diverted religion into speculative, and ultimately futile channels."[246]

It is likely that he received the degree of Doctor of Divinity in 1589.[247] A committed scholar, it was said that Andrewes knew fifteen languages, as well as the ancient languages of the Christian tradition: Latin, Greek, Hebrew, Aramaic, Syriac, and Arabic.[248] He was elected a Fellow of Pembroke College in 1578, and later became Master. He served in the London parishes of St. Giles Cripplegate and St. Paul's Cathedral. His parish ministry and especially his preaching brought him to the attention of Queen Elizabeth I who offered him the bishoprics of Salisbury and Ely, but Andrewes turned them down. He became Dean of Westminster under the old queen in 1601, but it was under the Stuart King James I that Andrewes became Bishop of Chichester in 1605, of Ely in 1609, and of Winchester in 1619. As Dean of Westminster he would have been caught up in the preparations for the coronation of that first Stuart monarch who showed him such favor, as well as with the funeral of Elizabeth I. He was often a preacher at court. The royal favor enjoyed under King James I has led one author to remark that "[Andrewes's] holiness was not immune from an interest in rich revenues," though it is only fair to acknowledge that Andrewes's considerable income was spent on assisting the poor and in educating the clergy of his time.[249]

He participated in 1604 in the Hampton Court Conference presided over by King James I, an attempt to mediate some of the differences between the English bishops and the Puritans concerning ecclesiology and liturgy. One of the outcomes of the conference was the authorization of a new translation of the Bible by King James, and Andrewes was given responsibility for translating the Pentateuch and the historical books, from Genesis to 2 Kings, doubtless due to his well-established competence in Hebrew.

On the very day that Andrewes was ordained bishop, November 3, 1605, the existence of the infamous "Gunpowder Plot" was made known to King James. Parliament was to be blown up on the very day on which the new Bishop Andrewes was to take his seat in the House of Lords for the very first time. Needless to say, public opinion was shocked. Andrewes registered this shock and perhaps also something of the relief of his own narrow escape in his first sermon on the Gunpowder Plot—eighteen such sermons are extant—preached on Christmas Day 1605. Popular, ill-informed sentiment, and ongoing anti-Catholic feeling combined to paint a picture of the

Plot as having the Jesuits behind it. The Jesuits, it was alleged, had given absolution before the event to those who had determined to blow up the King and Parliament. This was not the case. In fact, Fr. Henry Garnet, the Jesuit superior in England, heard about the conspiracy and did all in his power to persuade the conspirators to abandon it.[250] Reflecting the popular sentiment of his time, Andrewes said in his sermon:

> This abomination of desolation was undertaken with a holy oath, bound with the holy Sacrament—that must needs be in "a holy place," warranted for a holy act tending to the advancement of a holy religion, and by holy persons called by a most holy name, the name of Jesus . . .[251]

The irony is overwhelming. One response on the part of King James to the plot was the imposition of a new Oath of Allegiance. Cardinal Robert Bellarmine was instructed by the Pope to draw up a response to this oath, and Andrewes was instructed by the King to reply to Bellarmine. This is the famous 1610 *Response to the Apology of Cardinal Bellarmine.*

There is no evidence that Andrewes ever left England, ever traveled to continental Europe. Nonetheless, his geographical insularity had no parallel in his theology. "His view of the Church was consistently catholic and inclusive, and the Church itself he always saw as set within the context of the whole human family."[252] His theological work extended to apologetics and, as mentioned, he was engaged in debate with Cardinal Robert Bellarmine in 1609–10. He was a friend of the priest-poet-mystic George Herbert. Andrewes died in 1626 during the reign of the ill-fated King Charles I and was buried in what was then St. Saviour's Church and is now Southwark Cathedral. Over the years, the exact location of Andrewes's tomb in the church has been moved, due to renovation and other building needs in its vicinity. As a result, the tomb is now close to the high altar in the cathedral, and Bishop Kenneth Stevenson aptly comments that "Andrewes would probably like being so near a high altar because he was above all a man of the eucharist."[253]

Liturgical Architecture

"The idea of 'beauty in holiness' was a powerful motivating force in the development of early Stuart ecclesiology."[254] Concern was most obviously and especially with the beauty of the liturgy itself, but it did not stop there. A strong sacramental sensibility led also to liturgical architecture and furnishings. One fine example is East Knoyle parish church in the 1630s. The rector was Dr. Christopher Wren (father of the architect of the same name), and his theological formation came largely from Lancelot Andrewes, who had become his intimate and good friend. The plaster decorations made in the chancel "are shot through with Andrewesian theology."[255]

For a start, it seems clear that the Eucharist was being celebrated monthly rather than four or five times a year as had been the prior norm. The fact that the decorations were in the chancel indicate a strong sense that this was the place of communion with God. On one wall of the chancel Jacob's ladder may be found (Gen 28), the ladder from heaven to earth, with angels going up and coming down. The implication is that the chancel is the place, we might say, where heaven comes down to earth sacramentally, and where the communicants are taken up to heaven in virtue of their eucharistic divinization. Andrewes had created a new rite for the consecration of Jesus Chapel, Southampton in 1620 with the first reading being Genesis 28:10–22, and Christopher Wren was present on that occasion. He was impressed with Andrewes's theology and liturgical understanding. The Ascension of the Lord is depicted on the other wall of the chancel. This is especially interesting because Andrewes's Easter Day sermon in 1622 was not particularly on the Resurrection so much as the Ascension. At the time, Wren was Andrewes's chaplain and thus would have been very familiar with the sermon. Taking as his text John 20:17, Andrewes focuses on the Ascension as the *telos* of the Resurrection. Christ is the model for Christians. Christians rise from sin, a first Resurrection, and live Christ-oriented lives. They experience too, a first Ascension in that in this life their minds ascend towards God. There is a second Resurrection for Christians and all people at the end of time, but there is also a second Ascension for those who have let their minds and hearts ascend to God during life.

> While we are not at *ascendi* yet [that is, in body *ascended*] we be, for all that, at *ascendo* [that is, *ascend* in mind] ever as Christ here did. And *Blessed* is the man [says the Psalm] *cui in corde ascensiones*, that *has the ascension in his heart*, or his *heart* on it; That while it is *nondum ascendi* with him, yet at times it is *ascend*, lifts up his *eyes*, sends up his *sighs*, exalts his *thoughts* otherwhile, represents [as Christ does] anticipates the *ascension*, *Volo & desiderio* in will and desire, before the time itself will come of the last and final *ascension*.[256]

Furthermore, Andrewes goes on to point out that in John 20:17 the words are to be understood as so many rungs on Jacob's ladder by which we may ascend like the angels to heaven.

Preaching the Word

Lancelot Andrewes is not much studied these days both because of his language and his homiletic style. In respect of his language it has been noted that "Most modern critics . . . fix upon the bishop's sensitivity to the ranges of linguistic registers, his delight in the symmetrical division of texts, and his fondness for multiple meanings, metaphor, punning and multi-lingualism."[257] This is to be expected of a man with the linguistic skills and versatility of Andrewes, and most contemporary students of English lack much of the apparatus needed to access the inner reaches of his language and the theology found through it. While Owen Chadwick is surely right to say that "No one can now preach Andrewes' sermons," we can surely learn much from them.[258] Today's style is different, the rhetoric is different, and most of all the assembly that hears today's sermons is *very* different. Andrewes's biblical allusions, word-crafting, and exegesis would be lost on most English-speaking people in today's ecclesial world. Nicholas Lossky, son of the émigré Russian Orthodox theologian Vladimir Lossky, wrote an outstanding book on Andrewes's preaching.[259] Lossky is especially appreciative of Andrewes's patristic learning mediated in his sermons. More recently, the Episcopalian priest/biblical scholar, Ellen F. Davis, has turned her attention to Andrewes as something of a model for contemporary preaching: "The sermons of Lancelot Andrewes are unparalleled in the history of Anglican preaching for their comprehensive instruction in the basic understandings and practices of Christian living."[260]

Andrewes had a comprehensive grasp of the Christian tradition. Beginning with the Old and New Testaments in Hebrew and Greek, he was also familiar with both Latin and Greek patristic authors. He knew something of medieval theological scholarship, though it is not so much cited. He had absorbed the tradition in such a way that, as Donald Allchin remarks, "It is so living a thing, so large an element in our life that it becomes part of ourselves. We know with the whole of ourselves, become people who are caught up into what we know and are changed by it."[261] His knowledge of the Scriptures and of theology caught him up in this great organic tradition so that through his preaching he in turn could catch others up in it. "He speaks from tradition; tradition speaks through him."[262] At the same time, one must not see in Andrewes a pelagian approach to preaching, as it were. He uses his own vast erudition and linguistic *finesse,* of course, but he is no less certain of God's grace at work in and through his words. "The preacher allows the power of the Word and the direction of God to flow through the sermon . . ."[263] Andrewes knew that he was dependent upon God for the accomplishment of the homiletic task.

As tradition speaks through him, it speaks in a particular way. One of Andrewes's great gifts was to make words work. His linguistic aptitude and skills gave him the ability to do things with words in preaching that invited his hearers into a deeper appreciation of the mystery. A fine example is from the Immanuel section of his Nineteenth Sermon on the Nativity:

> And now, to look into the name. It is compounded, and to be taken in pieces. First, into *Immanu* and *El;* of which, *El* the latter is the more principal by far; for *El* is God. . . . For the other, *Immanu;* though *El* be the more principal, yet I cannot tell whether it or *Immanu* is our right to his might. . . . This *Immanu* is a compound again; we may take it in sunder into *nobis* and *cum;* and so then we have three pieces. 1. *El,* the mighty God; 2. and *anu,* we, poor we—poor indeed if we have all the world beside if we have not him to be with us; 3. and *Im,* which is *cum,* and that *cum* in the midst between *nobis* and *Deus,* God and us—to couple God and us. . . . If we have him, and God by him, we need no more; *Immanu-el* and *Immanu-all.* . . . Then if this be our case that we cannot be without him, no remedy then but to get a *cum* by whose means *nobis* and *Deus* may come together again. And Christ is that *Cum* to bring it to pass. . . . So upon the point, in these three pieces there be three persons; so a second kind of Trinity—God, we, and Christ. *El* is God, *anu* we; for Christ nothing left but *Im,* that is *Cum,* or "with". For it is he that maketh the unity in this Trinity; maketh God with us, and us with God; and both, in and by him, to our eternal comfort and joy.[264]

There is evidence that some of his auditors did not fully appreciate this kind of word-crafting on Andrewes's part, but it seems to be nothing other than the monastic practice of *lectio divina,* "divine reading," spoken aloud in a sermon. The poet, T. S. Eliot, a great admirer of Lancelot Andrewes, has it right when he says: he takes each word "and derives the world from it; squeezing and squeezing the word until it yields a full juice of meaning which we should never have supposed any word to possess."[265] A more brief and concise appreciation *of lectio divina* would be hard to find.

A more straightforward experience of his liturgical word-crafting is available in Andrewes's Ash Wednesday sermon, probably delivered on March 1, 1620. The text is Joel 2:12–13, "Therefore also, now [sayeth the Lord] turn you unto me, with all your heart, and with fasting, and with weeping, and with mourning. And rend your heart, and not your clothes, and turn unto the Lord your God." In this sermon the verb "turn" or its cognates are used 149 times. Ash Wednesday is about taking our turning to God with great seriousness. We must turn to God; turn away from our sins; return to God with all our heart; turn to God with fasting because "our repentance is to be incorporate into the body, no less than the sin was";[266] turn to God with weeping for our sins; turn to God with mourning. And, of course, Ash Wednesday takes us immediately to the holy season of Lent in which all these turnings are played out.

Lent and Penance

In an older register of discourse a penitentiary was a priest charged with responsibility for the Sacrament of Penance in a particular place. Through his attachment to St. Paul's Cathedral in London, an office that had associated with it the role of penitentiary, Andrewes spent part of each day during Lent in the cathedral making himself available for individual guidance and counseling. With the Reformation, however, the Catholic practice of confession of sin had undergone both criticism and change.

> While he held this place, his manner was, especially in Lent time to walk daily at certain hours in one of the aisles of the church, that if any came to him for spiritual advice and comfort . . . he might impart it to them. The custom being agreeable to the Scripture and Fathers, expressed and required in a sort in the Communion Book, not repugning the XXXIX Articles, and no less approved by Calvin in his Institutions, yet was quarreled with by divers . . . as a point of Popery.[267]

These are the words of a contemporary, Sir John Harington, and we may see in them the fine ecclesial posture privileged by Andrewes. The traditional Catholic practice of confession of sin, allied to spiritual direction, was what Andrewes was after. At the same time, the practice fell within the parameters established by the Book of Common Prayer and the Anglican

Thirty-nine Articles of Religion. "He relied upon the form of private confession and absolution contained in the Prayer Book form for the Visitation of the Sick, and which was [and still is] commended in the first Exhortation in the Communion Service."[268] Even acknowledging this rooting in the Book of Common Prayer, there were those eager to see in Andrewes's practice a predilection for the theology of Rome. Later, in 1600, on the Sunday after Easter when he was preaching before the royal court, he emphasized the need for private confession of sin, a sermon that proved to be somewhat controversial.[269] If one were to situate Andrewes on this issue he is certainly closer to Rome than to Geneva. Nevertheless, his commitment to confession and absolution remained firmly Anglican.

The Sacrament of Baptism

Andrewes had a firm grasp of the Catholic doctrine of grace, the patristic doctrine of deification, that God became one of us so that we might share in divinity. "He is in us and we in him, we and Christ are made one, we receive him and he receives us. So that as God cannot hate Christ, so he cannot but love us, being engrafted into him."[270]

This becoming partakers in the divine nature results primarily from the sacraments beginning with baptism:

> By regeneration in baptism, for except ye be born again of water and of the Holy Ghost . . . and by eating and drinking in the sacrament: in which the Apostle saith that we must "drink the Spirit" (*bibere Spiritum*) (1 Cor. 12:13). In this life we must seek for God's grace and glory; and he hath promised to give both (Ps. 84) and then we shall "enter into the joy of the Lord" (*intrare in gaudium Domini*) (Matt. 25); and we shall be always with him (1 Thess. 4); and see him as he is (1 John 3), that is be partakers of the divine nature; and which goes beyond all, he shall not be glory in one and joy in another and immortality in a third, but he shall be "all in all" (*omnia in omnibus*) (1 Cor. 15:28).[271]

Baptism, of course, is the first of the sacraments of initiation and is to be related to the terminal sacrament of initiation, the Eucharist. This is not the way Andrewes expresses himself, but he has the meaning:

> To baptism we may not come again . . . so out of it to apply to us, another way; as it were in supplement of baptism . . . in whom he receiveth so, to his table, to eat and drink with him, . . . with them

> he is well pleased again, certainly. On this day of the Spirit, every
> benefit of the Spirit, is set forth and offered to us; and we shall
> please him well, in making benefit of all. Specially to this, the only
> means, to renew his complacency, and to restore us thither, where
> our baptism left us.[272]

Baptism may be celebrated but once, as we are incorporated into Christ.
But that Christ-life requires supplement as we move through our earthly
pilgrimage. The supplement is the Eucharist. In receiving the divine supplement the Holy Spirit makes us "complacent," that is "pleasing" to God. The
Eucharist both heals and restores us.

According to the Orthodox theologian, Nicholas Lossky, Andrewes's
best sermons are the ones preached at Pentecost.[273] They show us something
of Andrewes's pneumatology both in respect of Whitsun and of baptism.
In the 1612 sermon Whitsun is the "Feast of the Holy Ghost" and it is also
the "Feast of Baptism": "For here is the whole Trinity in person. The Son in
the water, the Holy Ghost in the dove, the Father in the voice." He relates
this Trinitarian event to the primary Trinitarian event of creation in the first
chapter of Genesis. There the Father creates with the Word, by which everything comes into being, and the Spirit is brooding over the waters. Old
creation at the beginning of time, new creation through baptism. As the Holy
Spirit *manifests* Christ as the Son of God on the occasion of his baptism, so
the Holy Spirit *makes* humankind children of God when they are baptized.[274]

The Eucharist

As one would expect of a theologian standing, at least partly, in the Reformation tradition, there is a strong theology of the Word in Andrewes, as we
have seen. However, it is never at the expense of the Eucharist. Word and
Eucharist must be held together.

> To go to the word and flesh together. . . . But at this now, we are
> not to content ourselves with one alone; but since he offers to
> communicate himself both ways, never restrain him to one. The
> word we hear is the abstract of the *Verbum*; the Sacrament is the
> antitype of *caro,* his flesh. What better way than where these are
> actually joined, actually to partake them both? . . . Grace and truth
> now proceeding not from the Word alone, but even from the flesh
> thereto united; the fountain of the Word flowing into the cistern
> of his flesh, and from thence deriving down to us this grace and
> truth, to them who partake him right.[275]

It is entirely legitimate to interpret Andrewes in such passages as looking back to the best of pre-Reformation eucharistic theology, but also to the best of the Reformers. Word and Eucharist, with the Word interestingly as a fountain flowing into the Eucharist to feed humankind. Word and Eucharist are indissoluble for him.

Andrewes held a high theology of the Eucharist. He emphasized the real presence of Christ and the sacrificial dimension of the sacrament. In one sermon he picks up the famous inaugural vision of the prophet Isaiah in which the seraph comes to touch Isaiah's lips with a burning coal, and he sees the coal as a type of the Eucharist.

> In the liturgy of the ancient Church, these words are found applied to the Blessed Sacrament of Christ's body and blood.... [This sacrament] as Christ saith is nothing else "but a seal and signe of his blood that was shed for many for the remission of sins" (Matt. 26:28).[276]

There are different ways to come to Christ but the sacraments of the church are central for Andrewes, and the Eucharist is the center of the sacraments:

> There are different sorts of coming: first, we are said to come to Christ in baptism (Mark 10).... Secondly in prayer, for as Augustine saith *precibus non passibus itur ad Deum*. Thirdly in the hearing of the word. Fourthly by repentance ... but Christ receiveth none of these but that we come to him as he is *panis vitae*; when we come to Christ as he offers himself in the sacrament to be the lively food of our souls ..."[277]

The celebration of the Eucharist is the highest, most perfect encounter of faith with the living Christ, "for when we have the body and blood of Christ in our hands, then it makes us say with Thomas ... 'My Lord and my God.'"[278] In his Christmas sermon of 1615, the eucharistic Christ is the present experience of the Bethlehem Christ: "Here is the 'true bread of life that came down from Heaven' ... and where that bread is there is Bethlehem for ever."[279]

Towards the end of a Christmas sermon Andrewes speaks in a powerfully Irenaean fashion about the meaning of the Eucharist:

> There [at the altar] we do not gather to Christ or of Christ, but we gather Christ himself; and, gathering him we shall gather the tree and fruit and all upon it. For, as there is a recapitulation of all in heaven and earth in Christ, so there is a recapitulation of all in Christ in the holy sacrament. You may see it clearly. There is in Christ the Word eternal, for things in heaven; there is also flesh, for things on earth. Semblably, the sacrament consisteth

> of a heavenly and of a terrene part [it is Irenaeus's own words];
> the heavenly—there the Word too, the abstract of the other; the
> earthly—the element. And in the elements, you may observe there
> is a fullness of the seasons of the natural year; of the corn-flour or
> harvest in the one, bread; of the wine-press or vintage in the other,
> wine. And in the heavenly, of the wheat-corn whereto he compa-
> reth himself—bread, even the Living Bread that came down from
> heaven; the true Manna, whereof we may gather each his gomer.
> And again, of him, the true Vine as he calls himself—the blood of
> the grapes of that vine.

The Eucharist is here for Andrewes everything it would be for a Catholic,
but he wishes to underscore the earthly, material reality that is "taken up"—
or, to use a favorite word of St. Irenaeus of Lyons, "recapitulated"—in the
Eucharist. Earthly things are of importance to human beings, but they are
never "merely" earthy. They may in Christ become images of heaven. A. M.
Allchin says of this beautiful passage: "Andrewes in no way wishes to di-
minish belief in the real presence of Christ in the sacrament. On this point
he is at one with his Roman Catholic adversaries. But he believes that there
is a way of understanding the Eucharist which will do justice to the reality
of the gifts offered by man . . . more fully in accord with the proportion of
faith than a way of understanding which to him at least seems to deny or to
undervalue the earthly aspect of the sacrament."[280]

In 1610, at the suggestion of King James I, Andrewes published his
Response to Cardinal Bellarmine. Bellarmine had written a polemical work
suggesting that the Church of England was no church at all, and James had
requested Andrewes to respond. The *Response* has been described by the
liturgist-Bishop Kenneth Stevenson in these words: "Andrewes' reply reads
like a Bentley car driving along with effortless style, huge amounts of power
in reserve, and a faultless engine."[281] Even allowing for Bishop Stevenson's
hyperbole, there is beauty and persuasion in the *Response.* Against Cardinal
Bellarmine's assertion that there is no belief in the real eucharistic presence of
Christ in the Church of England. Andrewes replied to the effect that English
Christians believed no less than Roman Catholics that the eucharistic presence was indeed real, but that they do not define the *mode* of that presence.

> We believe no less than you that the presence is real. Concerning
> the method of the presence we define nothing rashly, and I add, we
> do not anxiously enquire, any more than how the blood of Christ
> washes in our Baptism, any more than how the human and divine
> natures are united in one Person in the Incarnation of Christ.

Andrewes is referring to transubstantiation. The first part of this passage is well known, "We believe no less . . . nothing rashly." Few advert to the remaining section, but it provides the clue to Andrewes's distaste for transubstantiation. The blood of Christ washes away human sin, but *how* remains within the holy Mystery that God is. The reality of the Lord Jesus is one Person with natures both divine and human, but *how* remains within the holy Mystery that God is. The doctrine of transubstantiation does not exist for him in the early church, and is a late medieval invention, and it is patently untrue. "At the coming of the almighty power of the Word, the nature is changed so that what before was mere element now becomes a Divine Sacrament, the substance nevertheless remaining what it was before."[282]

He viewed transubstantiation not as an expression in faith of Christ's total eucharistic presence, but rather as a rational, metaphysical explanation of that presence. Just as any rational, metaphysical explanation of the saving grace of baptism or of the person of the Word made flesh is impossible, so too with the Eucharist. Acknowledge, accept, and receive this eucharistic presence of Christ, but seek no rational explanation would have been Andrewes's position.

Further, Andrewes maintained that the Church of England held on to a Catholic understanding of eucharistic sacrifice:

> Our men believe that the Eucharist was instituted by the Lord for a memorial of himself, even of his Sacrifice, and, if it be lawful so to speak, to be a commemorative sacrifice, not only to be a Sacrament for spiritual nourishment. . . . Do you take away from the Mass your transubstantiation; and there will not long be any strife with us about the Sacrifice. Willingly we allow that a memory of the Sacrifice is made there. That your Christ made of bread is sacrificed there we will never allow.[283]

In this passage he demonstrates a clear understanding of the Eucharist as sacrifice, not in the sense of repetition, which was never the Catholic position (though it was often the perception of the Catholic position), but, in line with the earlier citation he entirely disallows the doctrine of transubstantiation.

Preces Privatae

It was said of Lancelot Andrewes that he spent about five hours in prayer and devotion every day.[284] The private prayers that he put together for recitation after communion reveal Andrewes's spiritual life. He made these prayers available to some close friends such as Archbishop William Laud not long before his death. They are not Andrewes's own personal composition, but rather "a glorious bejewelled patchwork of liturgical worship drawn out of the reserves of learning he had accumulated since boyhood . . ."[285] They are immensely rich in theology and in devotion, and they reach out to the entirety of God's creation. In his Sunday prayers of intercession, he prayed:

> Do Thou arise and have mercy
> on those who are in the last necessity.
> All in extreme age and weakness
> All tempted to suicide
> All troubled by unclean spirits,
> the despairing, the sick in soul or body,
> the faint-hearted.
> All in prison and chains, all under sentence of death,
> orphans, widows, foreigners, travelers, voyagers,
> women with child, women who give suck,
> All in bitter servitude, or in the mines, or in the galleys,
> Or in loneliness.[286]

Feel the power of this last line, "Or in loneliness." In these intercessions Andrewes has already prayed for the royal court and parliament, for farmers, for the fleet, and for tradesmen. These are the people on whom the commonwealth ultimately depends. But God's blessing must also be invoked upon those who are marginal to society, and his list of the marginal is truly comprehensive. In his Monday prayers of intercession we read: "Let us beseech the Lord for the whole creation; a supply of seasons, healthful, fruitful, peaceful." They reach out also to the entirety of God's Church. "For the Church Catholic, its confirmation and increase; Eastern, its deliverance and union; Western, its readjustment and pacification; British, the restoration of the things that are wanting, the strengthening of the things that remain."[287] This is a thoroughly ecumenical prayer. Andrewes prays first for the whole church. Then he prays for the Eastern Church, living with the burden of Islamic rulers. Notice that he also prays for the union of the Eastern Church, and one may assume that he intends both internal union among the autocephalous churches of the East as well as union with the churches of the West. Next he prays for the churches of the West, both Rome and the Reformation traditions. Finally, he prays for his own British Church, now united in some sense of the term under King James I. Donald Allchin rightly comments: "His own

Church is no less in need of the divine grace, which always heals what is wounded and makes up what is lacking, than any other."[288]

Conclusion

The Methodist theologian, the late Gordon S. Wakefield wrote that "[Lancelot Andrewes] became both in his own lifetime and in his subsequent reputation the embodiment of all that was best and most beautiful in the spirituality of the English Church."[289] Something of Wakefield's judgment, it is hoped, has been demonstrated in this brief essay. The cause of Christian unity cannot be well served until theologians and liturgists study carefully the "great cloud of witnesses" who have gone ahead of us. Without careful study of the past, and of one another's past, we shall remain fixed in our own theological and liturgical insularity. Bishop Lancelot Andrewes, at a very creative moment in the development of the Anglican tradition, mediates between the Reformation and Catholicism, and has much to offer those who love the liturgy and the cause of Christian unity.

10

The Liturgical Mystic, John Keble (1792–1866)

The re-birth of eucharistic piety is the most active of all the forms of fermentation which the Oxford Movement set working in the spiritual life of England.

YNGVE BRILIOTH[290]

JOHN HENRY NEWMAN REGARDED the 1833 sermon, "National Apostasy," by John Keble as the beginning of the Oxford Movement, the catholicizing movement in the nineteenth-century Church of England. In that sermon Keble denounced the British Parliament for suppressing, for various economic and political reasons, a number of arguably redundant Irish bishoprics. With a very high theology of church and episcopacy, he saw this state interference with the church as nothing less than apostasy, and it was this sermon that roused Newman to reforming action after his return to England from his Mediterranean trip. While many have heard of Newman and perhaps especially after his beatification by Pope Benedict XVI in 2010, fewer will have come across John Keble.

Who was John Keble? Born in 1792 at Fairford in Gloucestershire, England, to John Keble, the Vicar of Coln St. Aldwyn, the younger John Keble breathed in a High-Church atmosphere from the beginning. His father stood in a line of tradition that went back to the strongly liturgical Caroline divines of the seventeenth century, the High Church Anglican theologians who wrote mainly during the reigns of Kings Charles I (1624–49) and Charles II (1660–85). When his friends John Henry Newman and Hurrell Froude began to discover various forgotten strands of Catholic theology,

Keble in a sense had the upper hand. Thus, Georgina Battiscombe, Keble's biographer, writes: "When Newman and Froude were all enthusiasm for some item of Catholic faith or practice, which had burst upon them with the force of a new revelation, Keble would nod approval and remark in tones of highest commendation, 'Yes, that is exactly what my father taught me.'"[291] Keble stands theologically, liturgically, and spiritually in the great tradition of such divines as Richard Hooker, George Herbert, William Laud, Lancelot Andrewes, and Jeremy Taylor. Indeed, one historian of the Oxford Movement goes so far as to say that "Keble was the last of the Caroline divines and the Non-jurors; and the best of them."[292]

Having been a brilliant student at Corpus Christi College, Oxford, Keble was elected in 1811, aged nineteen, to one of the coveted fellowships at Oriel College, Oxford. Oriel was regarded as the most intellectual of the Oxford colleges at the time, and boasted a group of liberal thinkers known as the "Noetics," a group that was doctrinally liberal and highly critical of religious orthodoxy and far from congenial to the young Keble. Nonetheless, and this seems typical of Keble's personality, he seems to have got on well with the Noetics.[293]

He was ordained deacon in 1815 and priest the following year. Although he became a tutor at Oriel College in 1817, he left to assist his father in his country parish, and that was to be his life's work. Being a parish priest was his vocation. He moved on to a living at Hursley, near Winchester, in 1825 at the invitation of a former pupil, Sir William Heathcote, and, apart from some years when again he assisted his priest-father, he was there until his death in 1866. A very long and committed tenure as a parish priest! This is how Louis Bouyer puts it: "Though Keble was an accomplished scholar, he was first and foremost a man of prayer and the devoted parish priest of a small rural community."[294] The devoted parish priest was always his vocation. He ministered obviously to his patron, Sir William Heathcote, but most of his parishioners were ordinary working-class people, not known for their devotion to the liturgy and practice of the Church of England. The great Edward Bouverie Pusey, Hebraist and leader in the Oxford Movement, thought Keble's ministry a waste of his gifts and talents: "Through human mismanagement . . . the writer of *The Christian Year* should, for the chief part of his life, preach to a peasant flock, of average mental capacity."[295] Contrast Pusey's perception with that of a close friend and follower of Keble and later his biographer, Charlotte Yonge, who offers this fine description of his pastoral care: "The vicar was the personal minister to each individual of his flock—teaching in the school, catechizing in the church, most carefully preparing for Confirmation, watching over the homes, and, however otherwise busied, always at the beck and call of everyone in the parish."[296] Even allowing for some degree of hero worship in Yonge's description, is pastoral ministry to be counted a waste over against academic achievement in theology? Surely not, and perhaps that is not quite what Pusey intended. Keble must be judged an intellectual, but being an intellectual was subordinate to life in Christ. "To be clever was the gift of some, holiness was God's calling to all."[297] Keble was not to sever entirely his academic connection with Oxford, being elected Professor of Poetry in 1831 and holding this position until 1841. The Professorship of Poetry did not require residence, and demanded only four lectures a year. In Keble's time they were delivered in Latin.

Despite Newman's judgment about Keble's 1833 sermon and the beginning of the Oxford Movement, this is a controversial issue. Certainly, the sermon "National Apostasy" created a stir, but would it, or would Keble alone have been able to "create" the Oxford Movement? Certainly not, according to Owen Chadwick. Chadwick believes that Newman "charitably rendered Keble a disservice by hailing him as the true and primary author of the Oxford Movement. . . . Keble was the author of no movement."[298] Chadwick's judgment is surely correct, given all that is known of Keble. He was not the towering figure whose personal charisma and suasive rhetoric was capable of launching such a renewal albeit turbulent renewal movement in the Church of England. Yet, it must be said that Keble played his part, and a significant part. Not only Newman's words about the sermon "National Apostasy," but the testimony of virtually all who were caught up in the Movement bears witness to Keble's influence.

Historically, three men are commonly regarded as intimately associated with the inception of the Oxford Movement: Keble, Hurrell Froude, the passionate and somewhat radical thinker, and Newman. Each had his own contribution to make to the catholicizing of the Church of England, but they were quite different. Perhaps the historian Christopher Dawson gets it right when he writes of the trio: "Each of them played an essential part, but no one of them could have realized himself without the cooperation of the rest. Froude alone would have gone up like a rocket and left nothing behind him but a shower of sparks. Keble alone would have been a Conservative county clergyman who wrote pleasing religious verse. . . . Newman alone would certainly have done something, but who can say what?"[299] It was Froude who brought Keble and Newman together—the one good thing he said he had done in his life—and Keble took a key role in the Movement's publications. He contributed to the *Tracts for the Times,* the theological pamphlets promoting and defending the views of the Oxford Movement. After the *Tracts* had come to an end, Keble remained on good terms with Newman until the latter went over to Rome in 1845, and even then he felt a strong connection with Newman. After that, Keble remained in close touch with E. B. Pusey, trying to maintain the High Church emphasis in the Church of England.

In 1836 Keble put out an edition of the *Works* of Richard Hooker, one of the founders of the Anglican theological tradition. That year also saw Keble as Vicar of Hursley, near Winchester. There he remained as parish priest for the rest of his life. Ten years after his death, in 1876, Keble College, Oxford, was established in his memory, giving a sense of his very considerable impact on English ecclesiastical society.

The Mystic Keble

Bishop Geoffrey Rowell has it right when he says of Keble: "He had a natural sense of awe and wonder at the mystery of God, and a consciousness of the limitation of human language in speaking of God. He shunned ecclesiastical gossip and theological slogans . . ."[300] A fine accolade for any Christian minister! Writing elsewhere of Keble's spirit, the bishop says: "No blustering, no bragging, no knocking people over the head with dogmas, no thumping of Bibles, no multiplication of schemes and organizations—but an awareness that to worship is to adore, and that the prayer of adoration is the prayer of love, and that this inner core of our lives, our responsiveness to God, is a living out of a mystery, which always eludes our ability to express it in words."[301] Rowell's description leads one to suggest that John Keble was a mystic, even if in theologian John Macquarrie's words "a moderate mystic, a sacramental mystic."[302]

Even the most ordinary, daily, trivial experiences may have this mystical-sacramental quality to them, like sleeping and waking: "Every evening we do in a certain way, in the way of type and parable, represent and enact the mystery of Good Friday, and no less plainly, every morning we enact the mystery of Easter."[303] Nothing could be more ordinary, even trivial, than our sleeping and rising. But for the mystic Keble this is an existential participation in the Paschal Mystery. His moderate mysticism enables him to read all reality as charged with God's presence, but sinfulness clouds this vision:

> Two worlds are ours: 'tis only sin
> Forbids us to descry
> The mystic heaven and earth within,
> Plain as the sea and sky.[304]

The Christian Year, 1827

In 1827 Keble published *The Christian Year*, a volume of religious poetry built around the liturgical year as found in the Book of Common Prayer. One historian comments accurately, "What Keble set out to do was to provide a thoughtful commentary in verse to the Prayer Book."[305] It proved immensely popular, going through multiple editions from the date of publication until the year of Keble's death. Newman remarked of the volume: "Keble's hymns are just out . . . they seem quite excellent." Keble was as suspicious of popular Evangelicalism as he was of theological rationalism, but poetry mediated a sacramental sense for Keble—he dedicated *The Christian Year* to William Wordsworth—and his own poetry very deliberately so. Indeed, poetry and sacramental/mystical awareness are very close.[306]

There is no doubt of Keble's influence on Newman. As Geoffrey Rowell puts it: "If Newman came to hold so strongly that faith was communicated by personal influence, that 'heart spoke to heart' [the motto he chose when he was made a cardinal], then it was surely Keble who taught him so much of the priest who bears his people in his heart."[307] When it comes to preaching, there is a difference. While Keble's sermons are not in the same literary genre as Newman's, nevertheless his preaching was intended to provide the best of what the Oxford Movement had to offer to his working-class parishioners, a vision that is "profoundly sacramental, the visible world permeated through and through by the invisible world . . ."[308]

The Eucharist

"The liturgy is the divine script for a moral and spiritual drama, both the reenactment of salvation history and the actual enactment of personal sanctification."[309] Frequent celebration of the Eucharist was rare in the nineteenth-century Church of England, but Keble saw to a monthly celebration, moving later to a weekly celebration of the sacrament. He was up against the ways of the parish here. Despite his more frequent celebration of the Eucharist, and his equally frequent encouragement of his congregation to receive the eucharistic Christ, it seems that they were reluctant to do so. They were just as reluctant to heed his call for the sacramental confession of sin as a preparation to receive Holy Communion: "We go on working in the dark . . . until the rule of systematic Confession is revived in our Church."[310]

Two quite different scholars who have made a special study of John Keble's theology have reached identical judgments about his understanding of the Eucharist: Maria Poggi Johnson, a Roman Catholic historian of theology, and Geoffrey Rowell, an Anglican bishop and formerly professor of theology at Oxford University. Johnson writes: "Keble's views on the Eucharist are at the heart of his vision. . . . In fact, in his teaching on the Eucharist all of Keble's theological and pastoral thought comes together."[311] Rowell writes: "Keble's theology was particularly concerned with sanctification and it became increasingly a eucharistically centred theology."[312]

The celebration of the Eucharist involved for Keble a strong and passionate belief in the Real Presence of Christ. Maria Johnson puts it like this: "He takes every occasion that text or topic or season offers to press home both the reality of Christ's immediate presence where the sacrament is being celebrated and the immense importance of that presence for Christians."[313] No less was his belief in the Eucharistic Sacrifice. In the poem from *The Christian Year* entitled "Holy Communion," we find this stanza:

> *Fresh from th' atoning sacrifice*
> *The word's Creator bleeding lies,*
> *That man, His foe, by whom He bled,*
> *May take Him for his daily bread.*[314]

It is very clear in this verse that the Eucharist re-presents the unique sacrifice of Christ in such a way that this sacrificed Christ is taken in Holy Communion—"may take *Him*" for "daily bread." Both elements of doctrine, eucharistic presence and sacrifice, come together in this fine passage:

"For their sakes I am sanctifying myself, that they also may be sanctified through the Truth." . . . This one saying of Christ conveys apparently in itself the two chief points of the evangelical doctrine concerning the holy and blessed Eucharist: first, that it is His memorial Sacrifice, a means of obtaining God's favour and pardon for all such as truly repent: next that it is a most high Sacrament, a means whereby we are united to Christ, and so made more and more partakers of His righteousness here, and His glory hereafter. "I sanctify myself": there is the Sacrifice; "that they also may be sanctified through the Truth": there is the Sacrament.[315]

Like so many Anglican churchmen, Keble was opposed to Transubstantiation. Not to the belief in and acceptance of the Real Presence of Christ, but to what he took to be a too rationalist approach to the mystery of the Lord's presence. He was just as keenly opposed to those who would deny the Real Presence, as he says, "Wherever Christ is, there he is to be adored."[316] In fact, he sees both parties as being quite similar:

> Transubstantiation on the one hand, . . . the denial of Christ's real presence on the other. . . . The two errors in the original are perhaps but rationalism in two different forms; endeavours to explain away, and bring nearer to the human intellect, that which had been left thoroughly mysterious both by Scripture and tradition. They would turn the attention of man from the real, life-giving miracle to mere metaphysical or grammatical subtleties, such as our fathers never knew.[317]

He was a supporter of eucharistic adoration in the Church of England, and published a book, *On Eucharistical Adoration* in 1857, the work in which Owen Chadwick considers that Keble, who often declared himself incompetent theologically, "came nearest to being a theologian."[318] His basic position is that if the Incarnate Christ is the subject of our adoration, the Eucharistic Christ cannot be less:

> That, therefore, of which we eat, the same we are most humbly to worship; not the less, but the more, because in so giving Himself to us He is stooping so very low for our sakes. . . . If we really believe that which He declares to be His own Flesh and Blood is Jesus Christ giving Himself to us under the form of Bread and Wine, how can we help thanking, and therefore adoring, (for to thank is to adore), the unspeakable Gift, as well as the most bountiful Giver? seeing that in this case both are one."[319]

Sir Owen Chadwick, the *doyen* of church historians of nineteenth-century England, is our best lead into a somewhat controversial poem of Keble's to do with the Eucharist: "Froude believed the doctrine of the Real Presence and brought Newman to value it; a poem in Keble's *Christian Year* seemed to deny it. Even the closest of associates may sometimes contradict each other, and on matters which are not unimportant."[320] Chadwick is wisely saying that we ought not to look for exact uniformity even on important matters among the closest of friends, and, it may be argued, even within oneself. The poem to which he makes reference is as follows:

> *O come to our Communion Feast:*
> *There present in the heart,*
> *Not in the hands, th' eternal Priest*
> *Will His true self impart.*[321]

In the version first published in 1866 after Keble's death, the clause "Not in the hands" was changed to "As in the hands," thus making it consonant with Catholic theology. Taken at surface value, the original words suggest a much reduced version of the Real Presence, so that Chadwick describes this as "a near receptionist doctrine of the Eucharist."[322] John R. Griffin, in an unsatisfactory book that is far from the scholarly consensus on Keble, reaches the rather tendentious conclusion, based on these lines, that Keble did not actually believe in the Real Presence.[323] Griffin takes Keble's words with great seriousness, albeit in isolation from the total context of his life's *oeuvre*. Aligning myself with Chadwick—"[Keble] *seemed* to deny it"—it is necessary to say that there *seems* to be a contradictory element here in Keble's eucharistic theology. But the poem occurs in the early 1827 *The Christian Year*, some six years prior to his sermon "National Apostasy." If this poem is laid alongside his later views, especially in *Eucharistical Adoration*, it cannot be interpreted as his mature or final position, but must be seen as an intemperate expression of a eucharistic theology in progress. His eucharistic theology, along with so many other of his points of view, continued to develop.[324] That is what it means to grow and mature religiously. To arrest such theological development with one stanza from *The Christian Year* seems flawed.

Conclusion

The French Catholic spiritual writer, Léon Bloy, has wisely said that "There is only one sadness, the sadness of not being a saint."[325] By all accounts of those who knew him well, John Keble was a saint. As Bishop Geoffrey Rowell puts it, "If we would look for the secret of Keble's influence it is surely in that combination of magnetism and reserve, the hidden qualities of humility and holiness, that led his contemporaries to venerate him as something close to a saint."[326] However, he was a saint in his own tradition, the Church of England. This was something of a challenge to his friend John Henry Newman.

On September 12, 1865, when Keble had less than a year to live, the three old Oxford Movement friends—John Keble, Edward Pusey, and John Henry Newman—met for the last time at Keble's Hursley Vicarage. Newman wrote of the occasion: "There were three old men, who had worked together vigorously in their prime. This is what they have come to—poor human nature—after twenty years they meet together round a table, but without a common cause . . . and all of them with broken prospects."[327] They never lost their affection for one another. Writing from the Birmingham Oratory to Edward Pusey some seven years after Keble's death, Newman recalled words spoken in his hearing by Keble: "I think I have heard Keble say, 'Well, all I can say is, that, if the Roman Communion is the One True Church, I do not know it, I do not know it.'"[328] These sentiments were difficult for Newman, but it seems to me he regarded Keble as a saint. Newman viewed these words as demonstrating invincible ignorance on Keble's part, and thus, from his theological perspective, opening heaven to this self-evidently saintly man.

11

The Eucharist and Frontier Revivalism

Preaching builds up the faith of the congregation and magnifies it. Having heard the preaching, the congregation comes to the Supper in ever firmer faith and thereby celebrates the Supper to God's glory.

HUGHES OLIPHANT OLD[329]

KIMBERLY BRACKEN LONG IS professor of worship at Columbia Theological Seminary, Decatur Georgia. She completed her PhD in liturgical theology at Drew University and her dissertation has been published as *The Eucharistic Theology of the American Holy Fairs*.[330] To say the very least, this is a fascinating book and should be of interest to all who are interested in Christian worship, and perhaps especially to Roman Catholic liturgical theologians and ecumenists. The permeable boundaries of liturgy and ecumenism are best exemplified in the "high" sacramental churches and communities of the Reformation tradition. Outside this mainstream one tends not to think of liturgy and sacrament, but much more of a stress on Holy Scripture. This makes Long's research especially interesting, and so let us provide a summary of its central contents.

The Thesis

Kimberly Long's thesis quite simply is this: the roots of American revivalism can be found in the Presbyterian Scots-Irish sacramental occasions of the seventeenth and eighteenth centuries. These sacramental occasions on which the Eucharist was celebrated took the form of outdoor revivals lasting several days. These celebrations were held every year during the months between May and November when weather permitted those living in widespread rural areas to make the journey to their local churches. The celebrations included services of preparation, preaching and exhorting, as well as private meditation.

The week came to a climax in a communion service on Sunday and then came to an end with a thanksgiving service on Monday after which people returned home. Immediately, one is reminded of the structure of the Eucharist: Assembly-Liturgy of the Word-Liturgy of the Eucharist-Dismissal. These seventeenth- and eighteenth-century Presbyterian celebrations of the Eucharist, or, as they would have said the Lord's Supper, took the best part of the week—journey to the church, preparing seriously for the liturgical celebration, the celebration itself, the thanksgiving, and then finally the journey home. It must have been the case that for these Presbyterians great personal devotion and existential commitment were the essential preconditions for the celebration of the Eucharist.

Elements of Eucharistic Theology

A significant element of the Eucharistic theology on these festive occasions was the use of language from the Song of Songs, and other biblical marital imagery, describing the believer's union with Christ in Holy Communion. This is how Professor Long puts it:

> Close examination of the sermons preached just before the celebration of the Lord's Supper reveals yet another common characteristic: the frequent use of language from the Song of Songs to describe the union with Christ that occurs in the Lord's Supper. . . . The sacrament of the Lord's Supper is the place where Christ, the bridegroom, is wedded to the believer, the bride; it is the locus of a spiritual union that is longed for and experienced in part on earth, one that will be fully consummated in heaven. Central to this understanding of the Eucharistic Table as marriage bed is the use of language from the Song of Songs, as well as other biblical marital imagery, to describe this union.[331]

Some notes from the late 1760s by the Presbyterian divine John Beath describe some of the practices and experiences of these Communion celebrations: "There were some symptoms of the powerful and special presence of [the] God of grace, as everyone might discern and we can never enough be thankful for; it was a solemn, sweet, and glorious season; many of God's children were filled with the joys of the Lord and many poor souls brought to see their need of that Savior they had shamefully neglected, and wickedly crucified."[332] We may see in these words an emphasis on an experiential sense of God's presence. Furthermore, this experienced awareness of the God of grace gave rise to thanksgiving. This kind of language is characteristic of Catholic devotional and spiritual literature concerning the Eucharist and the Lord's presence.

Chapter 2 of the book is entitled "Mystical Union and Spiritual Marriage." It ranges from the Middle Ages to the eighteenth century. Catholic theologians and readers will recognize without much difficulty the mystical theme of spiritual marriage as this is outlined especially in Bernard of Clairvaux (1090–1153). Long also refers to the writings of Hildegard of Bingen (1098–1179)—arguably, one of the most impressive eucharistic ecclesiologists, though she would not have recognized the term necessarily —and the French theologian and conciliarist Jean Gerson (1363–1429).[333] Mystical union in these authors is often combined with strongly affective language, most frequently the language and imagery of spiritual marriage. For example, here is Bernard's understanding of spiritual marriage:

> What can be a source of greater pleasure than such a close union of wills? What can be more desirable than the love by which you, O soul, are not satisfied with human teaching, but go directly to the Word, remaining joined to the Word, familiarly relating and discussing whatever falls within the mind's grasp and the range of bold desire?[334]

Bernard is describing the spiritual marriage of the soul with Christ.

This language of spiritual marriage is not confined to medieval authors. There are continuities to be found between such authors and the Reformation tradition. Long notes that the boundaries between Catholic and Protestant authors on this point are not "as impenetrable as the polemics of the era suggest."[335] In fact, she maintains that prominent Reformation theologians continued with ease in this mystical union tradition of the medieval mystics. She goes on to describe passages from Martin Luther and John Calvin among others. Later on in the Reformation tradition the Puritans continued to use this language of mystical union/spiritual marriage, and she cites the late English Methodist theologian Gordon Wakefield to the effect that the Puritans were "not afraid to talk of rapes, ravishments and ecstasies."[336] Catholics would probably not associate this extravagant kind of mystical language with Puritan spiritual insight and practice. Having discussed the Moravians in this regard, Long naturally enough goes on to speak of the Wesleys in whom the Eucharist is described as "a soul-transporting feast" and "mystic banquet" leading to heaven.[337] Essentially she maintains, and I believe quite rightly, the traditional language of mystical union is being continued in respect of the Eucharist.

As she closes the second chapter, she says this: "What is interesting about the Presbyterian expressions, however, is that the focus seems to be more clearly on the Lord's Supper as the locus of this communion with Christ. Although the American Presbyterians would have been in line with Calvin—who, as shall be demonstrated in the following chapter, understood union with Christ to happen in a general sense as well as in the specific context of communion—the chief use of marital imagery and language from the Song of Songs appears to be in preparation for the celebration of the Eucharist."[338] Chapter 3 picks up this theme of mystical union in the theology of John Calvin and Theodore Beza. Those who read eucharistic theology in a broad ecumenical perspective will recognize one of Long's key resources in Brian A. Gerrish. While Gerrish was a professor in the Divinity School at the University of Chicago, he wrote a very persuasive and satisfying book on Calvin's Eucharistic theology.[339] Gerrish demonstrates that Calvin's eucharistic understanding was permeated by *Grace and Gratitude*, the title of his book. Long uses his work but in order to go further, in order to conjoin mysticism and Eucharist. Summarizing Calvin she writes: "Believers are united with Christ in two ways, one complete and one partial. Christ is first given in baptism, as believers are engrafted into the body, which is both the church and Christ himself. This union is once and for all, yet also effected over and over again, as Christ continues to grow and dwell in those who receive him" (44). This mystical union between the believer and Christ is a key element in Calvin's eucharistic theology. "For Calvin, the mystical union that believers enjoy with Christ in communion is as important as the union that is effected in baptism. In the meal, believers who are already engrafted 'into the body may grow more and more together with him, until he perfectly joins us with him in the heavenly life'" (45). She further quotes from Calvin's *Institutes* (4.17.32): "Now, if anyone should ask me how [the real presence of Christ] takes place, I shall not be ashamed to confess that it is a secret too lofty for either my mind to comprehend or my words to declare. And, to speak more plainly, I rather experience than understand it. Therefore, I here embrace without controversy the truth of God in which I may safely rest. He declares his flesh the food of my soul, his blood its drink (John 6:53–58). I offer my soul to him to be fed with such food. In his Sacred Supper he bids me take, eat, and drink his body and blood under the symbols of bread and wine. I do not doubt that he himself fully presents them, and that I receive them" (51). This is a very powerful passage. However Calvin might attempt to present an analytical understanding of Christ's eucharistic presence, there can be no doubt that he accepts it—"I do not doubt that he himself fully presents them . . ." When he says that he would rather experience than understand this reality, he may be pointing to what he regards as excessive intellectual analysis of this mystery of Christ present. When all is said and done, would it not be the case for most of us that we would rather experience Christ present than endorse a particular metaphysical understanding of the presence, however important philosophy is in the theological enterprise?

On the American Frontier

Long now gives attention to nineteenth-century preachers on the American frontier—James McGready and Gilbert Tennent, and then later to their theological and liturgical ancestor John Willison. She notes that this period known as the Great Revival saw a new form of worship emerging—the outdoor camp meeting. Various scholars have traced the relationship between the revivals of the late eighteenth and early nineteenth century and Scots-Irish sacramental occasions. This is how Long summarizes eucharistic themes in James McGready's preaching:

> A review of McGready's communion sermons reveals that two parallel objectives are simultaneously at work. One is to proclaim the gospel to unbelievers, who may be aroused by the Spirit, experience conversion, and come for the first time the Lord's table. Another—and equally important—objective is to perpetuate a rhythm of religious experience for believers, a rhythm of repentance, renewal and release that is acted out in rituals of exhortation, self-examination, and communion. The sacrament revival, then, is an occasion for both sinners and saints, where those who are already in the fold are renewed, and those who stand on the outside and looking in are urged to come inside (69).

Long makes the point that McGready's sermons are seldom doctrinal in intention, but he weaves sacramental language into those sermons, especially having to do with feeding on Christ and being fed by Christ at the communion table. When it comes to one of the more divisive issues in Eucharistic theology, namely the real presence of Christ, she cites one of his sermons in this fashion:

> Well, God is as really present at the sacramental table as he was in the burning bush at Horeb, or on Mount Sinai, or as he will be at the judgment of the great day. Then, as Moses did at the burning bush, turn aside and see this great sight, here you may behold all the perfections of God shining with amiable brightness in the face of Jesus Christ; you may view the infinite love of God towards our guilty race finding vent through the breaking heart and bleeding veins of the dying Jesus, and flowing to the chief of sinners ... (71–72).

In other words, Christians really do meet the real Christ at the sacramental table. In Long's own words "Worshipers came to the table to anticipate the banquet they would one day enjoy in heaven, and approached the sacrament as a little heaven on earth" (76). Surely this is as traditional a Eucharistic sentiment as one might find in the pre-Reformation tradition.

The Scots-Irish Eucharistic Inheritance

Turning in chapter 6 to the Scots-Irish inheritance, Long points out that sacramental occasions became central to the religious life in Scotland once Presbyterianism had become established by the end of the seventeenth century. A prolific and influential Presbyterian author, John Willison (1618–1750) has his preaching described in the following terms:

> [He] was concerned with teaching right doctrine to laypeople, using biblical sources as well as denominational standards to make accessible a Reformed understanding of the sacraments. He was equally committed to providing devotional materials that would aid people in preparing for the celebration of the Lord's Supper; his meditations led people through a process of self-examination and repentance, as they recalled the sufferings of Christ, reviewed the state of their lives, and prayed in earnest for forgiveness and renewal. Willison sought not only to remind people of Christ's sacrificial death and their need for repentance, but also to woo them to the Table and the union with Christ that awaited them in the sacrament. (107)

That particular verb "woo" has a very nice sound to it! It connects with the nuptial/spiritual marriage mystical tradition yes, but in ordinary human parlance it also has a soft and gentle tone. It has to do with inviting intimacy, the ultimate point of the celebration of the Eucharist. Willison argued for a more frequent celebration of the Eucharist, recalling John Calvin's wish for the celebration every Lord's Day.

By way of summary, Long notes four stages in the sermons and preparatory meditations of McGready, Tennent, and Willison:

1. "First, believers actively participate in a process of preparation through a prescribed pattern of prayer, meditation, and public worship" (131).

2. "In the second stage, ministers play the part of advocate in their preaching, urging believers to the Table on behalf of Christ. They woo them with the language of love, promising union, faithfulness, and the fulfillment of longing. In doing so, the preachers make use of biblical marital imagery, particularly the poetry of the Song of Songs, comparing believers to the lover/spouse/bride and Christ to the lover/spouse/bridegroom. The desire of believers for Christ is matched only by the desire of Christ for the believers . . ." (131–32).

3. "Third, there is the anticipation of union with Christ at the Table. In their sermons, the preachers point to the Table as the locus of that union; the Eucharistic Table is the marriage bed for the bride, who seeks to be joined with the Bridegroom in the sacrament" (132).

4. "The fourth stage is that of thanksgiving. After communion has been celebrated, there is grateful response in worship, in acts of charity, and in a renewed corporate life" (132).

And so Kimberly Long reaches finally to her conclusion, a conclusion that has been cumulatively built-up throughout her book: "The claim being made is this. In the sermons of American Presbyterian preachers involved in sacramental revivals, one observes theological expressions inherited from their Scottish forebears. These expressions are rooted in a solid Reformed theological heritage and are flavored with a strain of mysticism seen in medieval writers, one that is appreciated and in some ways reflected (if not imitated) in the works of John Calvin. Using language from the Song of Songs as well as other marital imagery, these preachers bring a Reformed mystical Eucharistic theology to a frontier revivalism that was once evangelical and sacramental. For American Presbyterians of Scots-Irish descent, the Eucharistic Table was a marriage bed, where union with Christ was experienced in anticipation of the final consummation in heaven, and believers who sought to meet their Bridegroom were ravaged with the love of Christ" (143).

Conclusion

One of the blurbs on the back of the book comes from Elsie Anne McKee, Professor of Reformation Studies and the History of Worship, Princeton Theological Seminary: "Stereotypes of the Reformed tradition are common. The idea that the Reformed tradition is a cold and loveless intellectual theology with an anti-liturgical bent is a popular caricature, and stereotyping rigid and frigid Puritans and Presbyterians in this way is a common practice. That makes this book by Kim Long especially enjoyable, because it demonstrates that the first generations of North American Presbyterians not only deeply appreciated the Lord's Supper but also expressed their devotion in the rich love-language of the Song of Songs." I read McKee's blurb after I had worked my way through *The Eucharistic Theology of the American Holy Fairs*. I think the blurb is entirely accurate, especially when it comes to Catholic perceptions of Presbyterian theology and liturgy. Appreciating the mystical-eucharistic insights of this rich book would go some way towards creating a more positive ecumenical-eucharistic climate.

12

Eucharistic Father and Son

Ronald C. D. Jasper and David Jasper

"This is my body . . . this is my blood." The words remain with us insistently, showing and inviting to the even deeper horror of consuming the elements, thus becoming one flesh with the flesh incarnate, dismembered and resurrected.

DAVID JASPER[340]

The study of liturgy and of liturgical theology received a great burst of energy from the changes brought about by the Second Vatican Council (1962–65), and this burst of energy was felt by all the mainstream Christian traditions. Resources for students became available, anthologies of liturgies were prepared, collections of essays on the history and the theology of liturgy were published. The early chapters of this book make ample use of one of these resources in particular, Ronald C. D. Jasper and Geoffrey J. Cuming, eds., *Prayers of the Eucharist, Early and Reformed*. This book was first published in 1975, and the third edition went into print in 1987.[341] It is a precious gift to students of liturgy, perhaps especially those beginning their studies, for two reasons: it provides the text of so many eucharistic prayers that would otherwise be relatively inaccessible; it introduces these texts with brief, but informed context and commentary. The editors, Ronald Jasper and Geoffrey Cuming were both priests of the Church of England with well-established reputations in the world of liturgical scholarship. This chapter will be given over to Ronald Jasper and his son David Jasper.

However, it would be remiss of me not to say a few words about Geoffrey Cuming.

One of the finest things that may be said of Geoffrey Cuming (1917–88) as a liturgical scholar is this: his liturgical scholarship went ahead as he continued with his priestly work. "[His] reputation has been mainly acquired in the classical tradition of the Anglican parish priest who quietly continues his studies amidst the daily concerns of his pastoral responsibilities. The bulk of Geoffrey Cuming's liturgical and historical work has not been done in the atmosphere of academia, but with the interrupting knock on the vicarage door always in prospect."[342] It would be most unfortunate for any church to lose this tradition of the scholar-parson. Cuming brought this great reservoir of ongoing liturgical research into the practical sphere of liturgical revision within the Church of England in the ongoing but necessary committee work. Cuming was no stuffy scholar whose liturgical researches, and at times speculations, removed him from the sheer practicalities of both designing and carrying out liturgies that drew people closer to God.

Ronald Jasper (1917–90)

It happened that on a cold winter morning early in 2011 that I received in the mail a volume entitled *Exchanges of Grace: Essays in Honour of Ann Loades.* Ann Loades is an English systematic theologian who taught at the University of Durham but is not especially well-known on this side of the Atlantic. This Festschrift contained a wide range of interesting essays, but one of them caught my immediate attention, "The Eucharistic Body in Art and Literature," and the author was David Jasper, Professor of Theology and Literature at the University of Glasgow, Scotland. I had come across some other works by David Jasper, but not anything on the Eucharist. So, the title of this essay was, to say the least, both intriguing and attractive. Then I wondered if this Jasper was related to another Jasper whose name is well known to students of liturgical and eucharistic theology, Ronald Jasper. The latter in concert with Geoffrey Cuming had produced for English-language students that excellent anthology of eucharistic prayers noted above. I found out that David is Ronald's son. So, this brief essay remembers Ronald Jasper and introduces David Jasper, especially for Catholic students of liturgy who may not know much about him.

Ronald Claud Dudley Jasper, an influential English-Anglican liturgical theologian, was born of working-class parents who were not especially interested in the church. It must have come as something of a surprise to them that their son was intent upon the priesthood in the Church of England. His biographer writes: "How and when Ronald discovered his vocation to the priesthood we cannot say. This was a personal matter, the details of which he never shared with his family. It was something very precious to him, a calling which he seems never to have doubted. In all his work he was always priestly without ever being pompous or parsonic."[343] That last sentence is a particularly fine description of a priest—"always priestly without ever being pompous or parsonic." He trained for the priesthood at Mirfield, run by the Community of the Resurrection, pursuing also studies in history at the University of Leeds. Ordained in 1940, he served initially in a coal-mining community, and then in a parish in Durham, giving him access to the University of Durham's Department of Theology. It was at this time that his interest in and research in liturgy began to develop in earnest. In 1943 Ronald Jasper married Betty Wiggins. He was soon appointed to a parish of his own, and one of his earliest visiting preachers was none other than the great Michael Ramsey, at that time the Van Mildert Professor of Theology in the University of Durham, and, of course, later Archbishop of Canterbury. Clearly, the young priest was interested in good liturgy and good theology, both interests being continued in his various pastoral placements. Working in pastoral ministry went hand in hand for the one fed into the other. His ongoing study of liturgy had to do with liturgical developments in the Church of England in the nineteenth century. These studies issued in a thesis presented to his old college, the University of Leeds, for the post-graduate award of Bachelor of Divinity in 1950. He was then invited to edit the papers of Bishop Walter Frere, an outstanding Anglican liturgist. Pastoral ministry and scholarly liturgical work enriched each other. As various pastoral possibilities were being made available to him, one of his clergy friends wrote to him: "So few clergy today have the taste or ability for study, that I should be sorry if you were hindered."[344] His friend need not have worried. Jasper continued to be a pastor, to study liturgy, and he also received commissions to write in the areas of ecclesiastical biography and history.

In 1945 Dom Gregory Dix, the Anglican Benedictine liturgical scholar published his justly famous *The Shape of the Liturgy.*[345] This beautiful book on the Eucharist fed into a popular liturgical movement gradually gaining ground in England at the time known as "The Parish and People Movement." This movement was much interested in promoting liturgical renewal in the Church of England and in the post-World War II years the movement was introduced to the Catholic liturgical movement including the work of such liturgical scholars as Lambert Beauduin, Olivier Rousseau, Louis Bouyer, Pierre-Marie Gy, Josef Jungmann, and Bernard Botte. These scholars were beginning to become household names in Catholic liturgical circles, but were now also having a very considerable ecumenical impact. The climate was such that there was a wide consensus that the time had come for a Liturgical Commission to be set up in the Church of England. It appeared in 1955, initiated by Archbishop Geoffrey Fisher, and Ronald Jasper was one of the primary members. The slow and cautious work of the commission was to bear fruit in the *Alternative Service Book 1980*, a liturgical revision to succeed the older Book of Common Prayer. One informed commentator says of him, "He was the chief architect not only of the *Alternative Service Book 1980*, but also of ecumenical cooperation in liturgical matters in the English-speaking world."[346]

Long before the *Alternative Service Book* was produced, however, Ronald Jasper's liturgical knowledge and ability were recognized through an appointment to teach liturgy at King's College London in 1960 and soon afterwards to become chair of the Liturgical Commission. Liturgy did not feature prominently in university departments of theology in the United Kingdom, but King's College had a developed a real respect for and academic location for the discipline. One of Ronald Jasper's most distinguished students from this period was Paul Bradshaw, a long-time member of the University of Notre Dame's liturgical cohort. Bradshaw writes of Jasper: "Had it not been for Ronald, it is highly unlikely that I would have entered the world of serious liturgical scholarship. Not only did he facilitate my admission as a graduate student at King's College London, and supervise my doctoral research thesis, but he was also instrumental in securing the publication of my early writings and in enabling me to take my first steps in teaching the subject."[347] Another outstanding student of Ronald's is Bryan D. Spinks, Professor of Liturgy at Yale University. Both Bradshaw and Spinks have written widely and well on liturgical subjects.[348]

Ronald Jasper's liturgical interests and responsibilities were amplified with the formation in 1963 of the ecumenical Joint Liturgical Group and with the invitation in 1965 to attend meetings of the Catholic Liturgical Translation Committee. It is little surprise, then, that in the post-Vatican II *Consilium* for the implementation of liturgical reform and renewal, when ecumenical observers were invited, the name of Ronald Jasper immediately sprang forth. Archbishop Annibale Bugnini speaks warmly of this ecumenical participation of the various non-Catholic observers: "They were the first to arrive at the meetings, the last to leave the hall. They were always affable, polite, sparing of words, and ready to engage in a friendly way in any conversation that might be requested."[349] Ecumenism was the way of Ronald Jasper. He was also early associated with the ecumenical and scholarly *Societas Liturgica,* the brainchild of a Dutch Reformed minister, Wiebe Vos. In fact, Jasper became the second president of the *Societas.* In terms of ongoing service to his Church of England he was a Canon of Westminster Abbey and then Dean of York.

In 1988 the Van Mildert Professor of Theology at the University of Durham, Daniel W. Hardy invited the now retired Ronald Jasper to teach liturgy in the Theology Department. The invitation had come at the suggestion of David Jasper, Ronald's son, who was now an Anglican priest, theologian, and Principal of St. Chad's College Durham. Hardy had been in the forefront of the renewal of the theology curriculum for ordinands and was keenly aware that liturgy too often was the Cinderella in that curriculum.[350] In response to the invitation Ronald taught liturgy at Durham for two years. Ronald Jasper died on April 11, 1990, Holy Thursday. His biographer comments: "Surely that is a poignant fact when we recall his lifelong concern for the dignity and rightful celebration of the Holy Eucharist."[351] Here was a priest for whom the celebration of liturgy was constantly accompanied by its study, a priest who was "always priestly without being pompous or parsonic."

David Jasper (b. 1951)

David Jasper, Ronald's son, introduces his essay, "The Eucharistic Body in Art and Literature," with some bold words: "At each new celebration of the Eucharist, and in obedience to the divine command, the body is displayed, eaten and consumed. The words are unequivocal—*this* is my body, *this* is my blood in the species of bread and wine, though there is a clear reference to the physical body of Jesus present before his disciples at their last supper together, now to be ingested by them as an act of remembrance."[352] The sheer realism of the eucharistic gifts is here expressed. Notice that he says the body is "displayed." Behind this strange usage of "displayed" here, lies an implicit but very real expression of the sacrificial cross with its tortured and stretched body. Operating with a high Christology—"in obedience to the divine command"—the eucharistic body of Christ is displayed, eaten and consumed (notice the further strong verb "ingested"). The act of remembrance is for Jasper no *mere* memory as though a shadow in contrast with reality. "To remember is no passive thing but a recreation in the whole of, and at the depths of, our being, a presencing . . ."[353] *Anamnesis* is never simply psychological recall but a new creation, "recreation," deep within us that can only be described as "presencing."

There has been, maintains Jasper, a recovery of the importance of the body in (post)modern thought, though he also thinks that Christianity has been somewhat ambivalent about the body, "perhaps inevitably given its focus on the cross." In this essay Jasper seems to be saying that the body celebrated in the Eucharist is, of course, the resurrected and glorified body of the Christ, yes, but it must first be appreciated as mutilated. This is a very costly body indeed. Perhaps we are less aware of the costliness than the sacrament demands. After using a number of artistic and literary references Jasper writes: "Art and literature continue to touch upon a barely conscious depth that Christian consciousness, nursed by theology, can barely comprehend in its narratives of resurrection and ascension, for it is only in a radical reversal of such consciousness, in an acknowledgment of the utter scandal of the body, that sacramental presence can begin."[354] This is not an easy sentence to grasp. What exactly is he saying? I hear him saying that Christian consciousness moves much too quickly to resurrection and ascension when contemplating the body of Christ. Theology nurses this move towards the glorified Christ and his body, and in a sense encourages and develops this move. But, to reach something of the sacramental presence of the eucharistic body there needs to be a re-appropriation of the mutilated and dead body of the Christ, "the body displayed is a broken body." There needs to be a retrieval of the pain and the scandal of the cross. Jasper goes on to say, virtually without contextual comment, "Into every Eucharist we die."[355] Jasper recognizes and accepts with the tradition, at least from the time of Athanasius of Alexandria, that God became human so that humankind may be deified, and that central to our deification is the Eucharist. Nonetheless, he asserts categorically: "But the suffering and the scandal remain—absolutely."[356] The suffering and the scandal remain absolutely but sacramentally. "The words remain insistently, showing and inviting to the even deeper horror of consuming the elements, thus becoming one with the flesh incarnate, dismembered and resurrected."[357]

There is more to David Jasper's complex essay than the emphasis I have drawn, but that emphasis is there. The costliness of the cross is folded into the costliness of the Eucharist, and to neglect that dimension is to sell the tradition short. Needless to say one could become overly obsessive with this dimension of the eucharistic mystery—the suffering, pain, the sheer brutality, the costliness of it all. But to be unaware is to neutralize all that emerges in those words of Jesus in St. John's Gospel: "Having loved his own in the world, he loved them to the end (*eis telos*)" (John 13:1), and his final word, "It is ended (*tetelestai*)" (John 19:30).

13

James Dunlop Crichton (1907–2001)

Liturgy does not lend itself to definition, but if one is to be attempted it could be stated as follows: it is the communal celebration by the Church, which is Christ's body and in which he with the Holy Spirit is active, of the paschal mystery. Through this celebration, which is by nature sacramental, Christ, the high priest of the community, makes present and available to men and women of today the reality of his salvation.

JAMES DUNLOP CRICHTON[358]

Introduction

ALTHOUGH HE SAYS THAT liturgy does not lend itself to definition, it would be difficult to better the definition provided at the head of this chapter by James Crichton himself. Although the book in which the definition is found is ecumenical, with contributions from scholars from different Christian traditions, and has gone through a second edition after its initial publication in 1978, Crichton's definition remains firmly in place. The reasons are not hard to find. Liturgy and ecclesiology are inextricably linked together; it is Trinitarian; and finally it is easy to grasp. It is the kind of thinking about liturgy that can only occur after many long years living it and reflecting upon it. That is exactly what James Crichton has done throughout his life.

It was in the living room of our house on campus at Newman University College, Birmingham, England, in the company of our pastor, Graham

K. Wilkinson, that I first met Msgr. James Dunlop Crichton in the early 1980s. I warmed to him right away, as we talked about theology and liturgy, and as he showed himself entirely at ease with our very young children.

Life and Context

James Crichton was a very private man, seldom speaking of himself or his early life. I do not recall Crichton ever mentioning his parents. Born on June 18, 1907, he went to school at Cotton College, the minor seminary for the Archdiocese of Birmingham. This is what he has to say about the liturgy at Cotton: "It was celebrated with great care and exactitude. It was something of an ordeal to serve the daily community Mass said by the headmaster, Thomas Williams, who later became Archbishop of Birmingham. By 1923 the whole school was singing the Ordinary of the Mass, in plainsong, alternating with the choir. Vespers on the greater feasts and Compline as well as other services were sung on Sunday evenings. The Holy Week liturgy, combined with a retreat, was very impressive. But when one went home for the holidays parish worship seemed all wrong. The contrast was glaring—and uncomfortable."[359] It was at Cotton that Crichton's love for the liturgy began to grow and where his lifelong emphasis on appropriate active participation in the liturgy first took root.

After Cotton, he proceeded to the major seminary, St. Mary's College, Oscott, and again he describes the liturgy: "Oscott . . . had a good liturgical tradition, though it was not at its best when I got there in 1925. It improved gradually, and the night office at Christmas, 'Matins' Mass and Lauds was a memorable experience for all that; by the end of it all, one was half-refrigerated."[360] The college and the chapel had been designed by Pugin. Though the buildings were undoubtedly very beautiful, the students were still complaining about the lack of heat in the 1980s when I taught theology there.

Crichton was ordained to the priesthood on May 21, 1932. He served at St. Chad's Cathedral for a year (1932–33), then at Uttoxeter in Staffordshire (1933–35); but it was only when he went to Acocks Green, Birmingham, in 1935, that he began "to try to get some 'active participation' from the people."[361] He arranged for a liturgical mission to be given in the parish by Dom Bernard McElligott. Crichton concludes about this part of his life: "I had been *doing* the liturgy before theorizing about it and it was not, I think, until late in the 1930s that I read Pius X's germinal statement, backed up by Pius XI 1928, that active participation in the celebration of the liturgy is the indispensable source of the Christian spirit."[362]

Crichton made good use of papal statements on the liturgy. In his motu proprio *Tra le sollecitudini* of 1903, Pope Pius X had maintained that active participation in the sacred mysteries of the liturgy was the indispensable source of the Christian spirit, and he encouraged the popular singing of the Ordinary of the Mass. Pope Pius XI, with his apostolic constitution *Divini cultus* of 1928, both strengthened and then carried forward the liturgical project of Pius X. In the constitution Pius XI urged the people to participate in the liturgy and not be "attached and silent spectators." Crichton soaked up these papal injunctions and did whatever he could to train people more adequately to participate in the liturgy.

Crichton had been appointed to the historic parish of Harvington when Pope Pius XII's encyclical on the liturgy, *Mediator Dei,* was issued in 1947. In this encyclical the Pope, like his predecessors, encouraged active participation, using the work of Robert Bellarmine to emphasize that the very structure and rite of the Mass demanded the response of the people. Crichton moved in 1955 to the parish of Holy Redeemer, Pershore, a village just a few miles outside the historic city of Worcester, where he was to spend the remaining forty-six years of his life. In 1958, Pope Pius XII signed and issued the last document of his pontificate, *Sacred Music and Liturgy.* This is how Crichton summarizes the document: "Its purpose was to regulate active participation at both High Mass and Low Mass. For the first time, it permitted laymen to read the epistle and gospel in the vernacular while the priest was saying them quietly in Latin. It allowed the singing of vernacular hymns during Low Mass provided they were appropriate and sung at the appropriate places (e.g., as entrance chants)."[363]

Vatican II's *Sacrosanctum Concilium/Constitution on the Sacred Liturgy* was promulgated in 1962, and in 1964 Crichton published his first book, a commentary on that constitution. Since 1964 a stream of books flowed from his typewriter—he never used a word processor or computer. He wrote and commented on every conceivable aspect of the liturgy: the Mass and the sacraments, the Liturgy of the Hours, our Blessed Lady in the Liturgy, the importance of Scripture and the liturgical year. The liturgical documents of the church were his constant friends.

Though rarely recognized throughout the academic world for his work, there were some moments of recognition. During the 1980s, Daniel P. Grigassy, OFM, received a doctorate a liturgical studies from the

Catholic University of America, the focus of his research being the pastoral liturgist, James D. Crichton.[364] On April 1, 1995, in response to a request made by the Liturgy Office of the Bishops' Conference of England and Wales, Crichton himself received a Doctorate in Sacred Liturgy, *honoris causa*, from the Pontifical Institute of Sant' Anselmo, Rome. He died on Sunday, September 2, 2001.

Theological Reflection on Liturgy

James Crichton never studied for a degree in liturgy, or a degree in arts or theology for that matter. A product of the English seminary system in the early part of the twentieth century, when it came to liturgy he was an autodidact. The primary influences that shaped his thinking were St. Thomas Aquinas, St. Leo the Great, and the texts of the Divine Office. Aquinas's treatise on the Incarnation, along with that on the redemption, provided him with the beginning of an appreciation of the Paschal Mystery. Crichton remarks of St. Thomas that, "At least he did not dismiss the Ascension in a scholion or treat the Resurrection as the occasion for apologetics."[365] He certainly did not think of St. Thomas as the final word in Catholic theology, though he knew his way around the *Summa Theologiae*, especially the *De Vita Christi* in *Pars III*, which "summarized so much of the patristic tradition on the life of Christ."[366] From Aquinas came his appreciation that the mysteries of Christ's life, for example, the Baptism and the Transfiguration, were not mere historical events in the past, but "mysteries" pregnant with meaning for the present.

If Aquinas laid the foundations for Crichton, it was Leo the Great who intensified his liturgical passion. Crichton had begun to read the sermons of Leo the Great as a student, and the very first book he purchased after ordination was a large folio volume of Leo's *Opera Omnia*: "As I gradually absorbed him I came to think, as I still do, that he is one of the best commentators on the liturgical year. He leads one to see that the feasts and seasons of the year are not mere commemorations but celebrations making present the great mystery of Christ."[367]

Of course, those were the days when the classics, Greek and Latin, were *de rigueur*, not only in seminaries but also in grammar school education generally. At that time there were few English translations of the great corpus of patristic literature, and not only English translations. *Sources chrétiennes* was just getting underway in France in the late 1930s and early 1940s. Giving papers to the Society of the Magnificat from the 1940s onwards, a society whose members undertook to say one hour of the office each day, required Crichton to study not only patristic texts but also the Vulgate, and to have an increasing concern for holy Scripture, including modern exegesis. He added to his studies historical treatments of the liturgy, naming especially Edmund Bishop, Louis Duchesne, Pierre Battifol, Herbert Thurston, Adrian Fortescue, and later, Odo Casel. It was this constancy of study in a pastoral ambience of regular liturgical celebration that provided Crichton with the apparatus needed to convey what *Sacrosanctum Concilium* was all about when it was promulgated in 1963. "If I was able to write my first book, *The Church's Worship* (1964), in something from eight to ten weeks it was because I recognized in it teaching with which I had long been familiar."[368]

Crichton knew all too well the problems and difficulties that liturgy faced before the reforms set in motion by Vatican II, but that never prevented him from recognizing the utter sense of reverence and devotion that was present. "However unsatisfactory the celebration (of Mass) was from many points of view, the people were aware that they were in the presence of God and that, at Communion, they were receiving into themselves Jesus Christ our Lord, God the Son. Their faith was strong and their professed it by what they did."[369]

Both as a pastor and as a lecturer constantly in demand on liturgical topics, Crichton traveled around the United Kingdom and sometimes in the United States. He realized that the liturgical reforms of Vatican II were not always and everywhere implemented with care and reverence. "It was fortuitous and perhaps unfortunate," he wrote, "that the Constitution on the Liturgy of the Second Vatican Council should have appeared in the swinging sixties, when there was developing a free-for-all in almost everything."[370] He was well aware of the problems. In architecture he knew that "some new churches became sheds for the celebration of a diminished liturgy," and in music that "poor quality folk music, of which both words and melodies were banal and egocentric," had displaced the great and popular tradition of English hymnody. In the celebration of the liturgy he decried the performance of the ceremonial of the Mass "in sloppy fashion," and the homily that had become too often "a shapeless chat."[371]

Nevertheless, Crichton refused to go along with the critique of Aidan Nichols, OP, in his book *Looking at the Liturgy*.[372] In a lengthy and, at times, somewhat harsh review, Crichton took Nichols to task for what he understood to be overstatement, inaccuracy, and a desire to return to the past.[373]

While Nichols found fault with the presuppositions of the liturgists who came in the wake of the Enlightenment, Crichton's own research led him in his *Lights in the Darkness* to see liturgical trailblazers not as propagating an ideology so much as being "soundly based in Catholic theology."[374] When Nichols comments that contemporary church architecture is suffering from "radical functionalism," Crichton stresses the radically functional nature of medieval monastic and cathedral churches, which were built "to meet the liturgical needs and duties of monks and canons."[375] He faults Nichols for getting wrong the title of the post-conciliar *Ordo dedicationis ecclesiae et altaris,* a document Crichton knew particularly well since he published a limited-edition commentary on it, primarily for episcopal use. He concludes that, "Things are not to be done simply because they were done long ago," even as he agrees that, "If celebrants do not know how to [celebrate] with reverence than they should be taught."[376] While there is much to do to improve the quality of liturgical preaching and celebration, to invite and to enhance awe and reverence in celebration, there can be no going back to the pre-conciliar position. If anything were to summarize Crichton's position on the reformed liturgy, it would be what is often spoken of today as the program of re-catholicization.

This is how the Bishop of Brentwood, Thomas McMahon, described the achievement of Msgr. Crichton:

> One cannot begin to quantify what a profound influence Msgr. Crichton has had on the renewal of liturgical life in England in nearly sixty years. It has been scholarly, drawing on the fathers of the Church and Scripture. It has been informed with tradition and liturgical principles of previous ages. It has been pastoral, through his own priestly ministry and experience as a parish priest. It has been lucid, since his writing and lecturing is always so clear, practical and incisive. All of this has been done in the most self-effacing manner and rather independent English spirit, with that special brand of dry humor that we have come to associate with him.[377]

That is a very fair and accurate summary. Crichton was a pastoral liturgist, a man for his contemporaries and a man of the church—in fact, these are the categories singled out for mention by Abbot Marcel Rooney in his *laudatio* on the occasion of the conferring of Crichton's honorary doctorate.[378]

As a pastoral liturgist, Msgr. Crichton loved and served his parish. The parish was his focal concern, the physical source for his liturgical research and its constant beneficiary. He typified the English model of the scholar-parson, as we have seen his Anglican contemporary, Geoffrey Cuming, also had done (in chapter 11). Study and celebration in service to the people of God went hand-in-hand. The Central Catholic Library in London was the recipient of many requests for articles and books, first in his parochial residence in Pershore, and then, after 1988, in his little "Norfork Cottage," also in Pershore.

Crichton sought to make the liturgy speak to his contemporaries, and he recognized that, at times, ecclesiastical institutions may get in the way of people's quest for God. The church, without intending it, can sometimes be a stumbling block or a scandal to people. Crichton appreciated this truth, all the while recognizing with mature wisdom that there was for a Catholic nowhere else to go. In a passage that Abbot Marcel Rooney describes as "brilliant," Crichton responds to the frustration of some contemporaries with the church:

> But what is the alternative? Even the purest religion of the word can degenerate into formalism, the freest form of prayer can petrify and large aspirations can vanish in clouds of unrealism. Either way, the seeds of human imperfection can mar the vaunting idealism of man. It is part of the human condition and he has got to come to terms with it. If he does, he should find that the material, the particular, the humble element can become for him a theophany. . . . There is a St. Francis to bear witness that the sun and the moon, fire and water, and even the humble body can in Christian eyes be the images . . . of divine Beauty. This, it seems to me, is as genuine an intuition of Being as is that born of the anguish that seems to have been the *point de départ* of the existentialists.[379]

Crichton wanted the liturgy to reach the contemporary person, because he realized from his faith and the great liturgical tradition that it was the primary way in which God was reaching out to our contemporaries.

Crichton was *par excellence* a man of the church, that is to say, of the communion of the church, of the community as the *locus* of the liturgy. He knew that "Christian prayer is radically communal. It is the prayer of the *ecclesia,* the assembly that is the body of Christ, and all Christian prayer is prayer in Christ and through Christ."[380]

Conclusion

I recall Crichton's response to a comment made by a mutual priest-friend about the liturgical assembly, the church. The priest had complained to Crichton that the local community could be so demanding, and that there were times when he felt the burden of demand almost overwhelming. Crichton responded: "Well, you'd better get to like it because that's what you're about as a priest." Crichton's entire life was about the local communion of the church, even when it could be burdensome. He was a man of the church. He once described the Italian liturgist, Lodovico Antonio Muratori (1672–1750) as a liturgical scholar and "a pastoral priest who took exemplary care of the people entrusted to his charge."[381] The description fits its author.

14

Graham Greene
and Monsignor Quixote's Final Eucharist

Quixote's final Eucharist is his life, an incarnate sign of the spiritual energy of love.

MARK BOSCO, SJ[382]

GRAHAM GREENE (1904–91) WAS one of the most accomplished novelists of the twentieth century. He became a Catholic in 1926, having undergone instruction at the hands of Fr. Trollope of the cathedral in Nottingham, UK. Many of his novels attend both directly and indirectly to broad Catholic themes. He understood himself to be a novelist who happened to be a Catholic rather than a Catholic novelist. "Whatever this might mean, and it is debated, what cannot be denied is the 'iconology of Catholicism' throughout his work. The icons are everywhere, as he shows religion (Catholicism in particular) to be a central influence in the lives of his characters."[383]

Greene published *Monsignor Quixote* in 1982.[384] It has been well described by an authority on Greene's works in these words: "Religion may win out in these (religious) novels, but flashes of darkness remain. Darkness, of course, is no bad thing. Darkness helps keep religion honest and perhaps alive. It is still there at the heart of *Monsignor Quixote,* by far Greene's gentlest book."[385] What an interesting description of the novel! I take the author of these comments, John Auchard, to mean that authentic religious faith, even as it grows in a person's life and leads the person into greater light, that is, into deeper communion with God, is also often characterized by "flashes of darkness." Equally, I take it that a person who lives out life in darkness over against explicit religious faith also experiences "flashes of light." Given the complexity of human lives, it seems impossible that the darkness of doubt, and certainly of fundamental and basic questions, can ever be completely eliminated. It is the frank acknowledgment of the flashes of darkness, according to Auchard, that not only maintains and supports genuineness and authenticity, but also keeps religion alive. "Alive" in this context can only mean absolutely real in terms of human experience, with not only its joys but also its deep ambiguities.

Such darkness exists, of course, in *Monsignor Quixote*, but we are told in the "gentlest" of ways. Gentlest, because the darkness, and I would say also the light, is played out over the growing love between two seemingly opposed men. The novel is about the deep friendship that arose between Fr. Quixote the parish priest of the Spanish village of El Toboso and the Communist Mayor of the village, Enrique Zancas, who is called Sancho by the priest. Fr. Quixote believes himself to be a real descendant of Cervantes's 1605 *Don Quixote de la Mancha*. The two set off in Quixote's ancient car, suitably named *Rocinante*, Don Quixote's horse in Cervantes's novel.

The two set off on a journey together. This is significant in terms of Greene's biography and also theologically. In terms of his biography the novel emerges out of many journeys in Spain, vacations of Greene with his friend the Spanish priest Leopoldo Duran.[386] Theologically, the Gospels tell us, each in its own particular way, of how journeying with Jesus was the living context of the disciples' growth in faith and understanding of Jesus. These journeys ultimately climax in Jerusalem, as they move towards the Last Supper and the death and resurrection of Jesus. As they journey, Quixote and Sancho get into all manner of unlikely and humorous experiences. The novel must be read right through to savor these experiences, but a nice summary is afforded by Mark Bosco: ". . . Quixote spends a night in a brothel, unwittingly views a pornographic film, hears a confession in a public toilet, and helps a thief escape from the police."[387] Not normal experiences for a Catholic priest! The journeying, the experiences knit the men more closely together in an ever-growing relationship—one really has to say in an ever-growing "communion", for that is what it is. This growth in communion comes about through the journeying, yes, but it is deepened and rendered more profound by their conversations and their dining together. It would be tedious to attempt a resumé of their conversations. They must be read for themselves. The conversations move both of them "onto more mysterious ground."[388] The conversations are seriously dialogical. Thus, for example, Quixote lends Sancho his copy of Heribert Jone's moral theology textbook, while Sancho invites Quixote to read Marx's *The Communist Manifesto*. Quixote comments on the book to Sancho: "But you've been my friend for a long time, Sancho, and I want to understand you. *Das Kapital* has always defeated me. This little book is different. It's the work of a good man. A man as good as you are—and just as mistaken."[389] While he appreciates the goodness of Marx, Quixote retains his judgment that he is mistaken. Sancho finds much in Jone's *Moral Theology* to laugh at. Quixote is careful to respond to his jibes with a certain respect for Jone, but, at the same time he says to Sancho: "You may laugh at Father Jone, and I have laughed with you, God forgive me. But, Sancho, moral theology is not the Church."[390] These conversations, these dialogues constitute a Liturgy of the Word, an anonymous but real Liturgy of the Word. Through these conversations, serious and funny, they are drawn more closely together in communion. They encounter the real presence of one another, and slowly that encounter is bringing about mutual transformation. This is not transformation in some kind of Damascus road fashion. Those moments seldom occur for most people. The transformation is virtually imperceptible as they open up through words. The meals they share are more like picnics than anything else. The picnics are made up of wine and cheese. They constitute a Liturgy of the Eucharist, an anonymous but real Liturgy of the Eucharist between the two companions. It must be recalled that the word "companion" means in its Latin roots, "to eat bread with," "to share a meal with." Perhaps we might say that the communion effected through conversation comes to its full manifestation in the joy and satisfaction of com-panioning, of eating and drinking together. Transformation. . . . The entire novel may be understood eucharistically, but this motif comes to its supreme expression in the very last part of the narrative. Mark Bosco has it exactly right: "Quixote's act of selfless love [in his final Eucharist] is itself a response to his compañero's gradual intensification of his commitment to him as both friend and priest. Only after Quixote is touched by their travel, conversation, and concern for one another is he finally prepared to recognize Sancho as his compañero. That bond is given a sacred signification in the concluding celebration of the Eucharist."[391]

Part IV, The Final Eucharist

This final section of the novel is entitled "How Monsignor Quixote Rejoined His Ancestor." The ancestor, of course, is the Don Quixote of Cervantes, who is believed by Monsignor Quixote to be his ancestor. In part 1, we have described for us the Trappist monastery of Osera in the Galician hills. The monastery buildings date back to the twelfth century, but they are kept in good repair, physically and spiritually. It is an ordinary place with ordinary people, but it is also a holy place, a place that invites communion. The monastery is the "upper room" for Monsignor Quixote and Sancho as they reach the end of their journeying together. But the other *dramatis personae* must be introduced before we get to this "Last Supper."

Part 2 begins with the description of a less than exciting lunch that had been prepared by one of the Trappist monks, Fr. Leopoldo. Here one recalls the Christian name of Greene's long-time Spanish priest friend, Leopoldo Duran. An important guest at the monastery, Professor Pilbeam, Professor of Hispanic Studies at the University of Notre Dame and probably the world's leading authority on St. Ignatius Loyola, had hardly touched his lunch, and Leopoldo feels ashamed. Leopoldo and Pilbeam stand in clear contrast. Leopoldo had found his way of out of skepticism into Christian faith with René Descartes as guide and mystagogue. His faith had taken him to Osera, though it had not given him any culinary charism. Pilbeam is in his own description a nominal Catholic. Unable to find Professor Pilbeam to make his apologies for the poor quality of the lunch, he goes into the chapel, where he often prayed for Descartes and sometimes to Descartes. There Fr. Leopoldo finds Pilbeam and they enter into conversation. If the professor could only find some lost document about St. Ignatius, he would die a happy man. As they converse, Pilbeam insists to the monk that he is interested only in facts to which Leopoldo replies: "Fact and fiction—they are not always easy to distinguish. . . . In the end you can't distinguish between them—you just have to choose."

"Fact" and "fiction" are the backdrop for this final act of the drama. But what are they? "Fact" for Pilbeam is something that is objectively verifiable. That is what constitutes the real for him. "Fiction" for Leopoldo does not admit of that kind of empirical verification, but nevertheless is a conduit to the real. It might be said that the real is for Leopoldo (and for Greene) something mediated, something sacramental, "what is real *within* and yet *beyond* matter."[392]

As this conversation continues, both professor and monk hear a loud noise, the former thinking that a tire has blown out with a resultant car crash, but the latter thinks that it was gunshots. In fact it was gunshots on the part of the police, the Guardia Civil, but gunshots aimed at the tires of a car whose occupants they were trying to catch. The car was carrying Mayor Sancho and Monsignor Quixote. Monsignor Quixote has been injured. Because of the injuries received by Monsignor Quixote, Fr. Leopoldo refuses to let the policemen take the two men away and the monsignor is carried through the church to a guest room where he will rest until the doctor comes to examine him. The doctor examines both his patients, the mayor receiving some stitches for a head wound, but the priest is given a sedative. The priest appears to be basically all right, not badly injured, but, given his age, he will need to be watched. And so the watch begins. Jesus's "Stay here and watch with me" in Gethsemane comes to mind but in a blurred way, because the Last Supper has not happened yet.

At one o'clock in the morning Monsignor Quixote tries to get out of bed, but his legs give out and he cries for help. Sancho and Leopoldo are there to assist him, with Professor Pilbeam looking in from the doorway to the room. Quixote is dazed, unclear about his whereabouts, and about what is happening to him. He thinks he is back in El Toboso, in trouble with his bishop and with his books about to be burned by the assistant priest. Fr. Leopoldo asks, "What books?" Quixote replies: "The books I love. Saint Francis de Sales, Saint Augustine, Señorita Martin of Lisieux. I don't think [the bishop] trusts me even with Saint John." It is very telling that one of his favorite books is Señorita Martin, aka St. Thérèse of Lisieux's "Story of a Soul" or her "Little Way of Love." That is Quixote's way too. Quixote's bishop was suspicious of his reading and has forbidden him to say Mass, even on his own. He is given another sedative and returns to sleep while Leopoldo and Sancho continue to keep watch. He re-awakens at three in the morning, again dazed and unsure of what is going on. There follows a brief but very strange conversation that re-plays some of the events from earlier in the book. Then Monsignor Quixote gets up and in a dream-like state moves from his room towards the church. Leopoldo and Sancho let him proceed, judging that to wake him might be dangerous, but they are right by his side.

He goes up to the altar and begins the old Latin Mass: "*Introibo ad altare Dei, qui laetificat juventutem meam.*" "I shall go to the altar of God, who gives joy to my youth." The Mass has begun, as it were, Monsignor Quixote's "Last Supper." Let's read the narrative in Greene's own words, but abbreviated.

The Mass went rapidly on—no epistle, no gospel: it was as though Father Quixote were racing towards the consecration.... "When he finds no paten and no chalice, surely he will wake," Father Leopoldo said. The Mayor moved a few steps nearer to the altar. He was afraid that, when the moment of waking came, Father Quixote might fall, and he wanted to be near enough to catch him in his arms.

"Who the day before he suffered took bread ..." Father Quixote seemed totally unaware that there was no Host, no paten waiting upon the altar. He raised empty hands. *"Hoc est enim corpus meum"* ["For this is my body"], and afterwards he went steadily on without hesitation to the consecration of the nonexistent wine in the nonexistent chalice ... *"Hic est enim calix sanguinis mei"* ["For this is the chalice of my blood."] The empty hands seemed to be fashioning a chalice out of the air ...

So it was he remembered the Our Father, and from there his memory leapt to the *Agnus Dei, "Agnus Dei qui tollis peccata mundi"* ["Lamb of God, who takes away the sins of the world."] ... "Lord I am not worthy that Thou shouldst enter under my roof; say but the word and my soul shall be healed." ...

For a few seconds Father Quixote remained silent. He swayed a little back and forth before the altar. The Mayor took another step forward, ready to catch him, but then he spoke again: *"Corpus Domini nostri"* ["The Body of our Lord"], and with no hesitation at all he took from the invisible paten the invisible Host and his fingers laid the nothing on his tongue. Then he raised the invisible chalice and seemed to drink from it. The Mayor could see the movement of his throat as he swallowed ...

He remarked the Mayor standing a few feet from him and took the nonexistent Host between his fingers; he frowned as though something mystified him and then he smiled. *"Compañero,"* he said, *"you must kneel, compañero."* He came forward three steps with two fingers extended, and the Mayor knelt. Anything which will give him peace, he thought, anything at all. The fingers came closer. The Mayor opened his mouth and felt the fingers, like a Host, on his tongue ... and then his legs gave way. The Mayor had only just time to catch him and ease him to the ground. *"Compañero,"* the Mayor repeated the word in his turn, "this is Sancho," and he felt over and over again without success for the beat of Father Quixote's heart.

Quixote and Sancho had been throughout their journeying *compañeros* to each other, and now, at journey's end, they are for the last time *compañeros,* eating the Eucharistic bread together. Through that eating, so to speak, they are both *Corpus Domini nostri,* "the Body of our Lord Jesus Christ," albeit in contrasting ways.

Was Monsignor Quixote's Final Eucharist the Eucharist?

The following day a conversation took place between Fr. Leopoldo, Professor Pilbeam and Sancho. The topic of conversation was Monsignor Quixote's Mass in the abbey church. What happened? Was it really the Mass, or not? Once again, it's better in Greene's own words, here slightly adapted to bring out the features of the conversation:

> Pilbeam: "There was no consecration. . . . There was no Host and no wine."
>
> Leopoldo: "Descartes, I think, would have said rather more cautiously than you that he *saw* no bread or wine."
>
> Pilbeam: "You know as well as I do that there *was* no bread and no wine."
>
> Leopoldo: "But Monsignor Quixote quite obviously believed in the presence of the bread and wine. Which of us was right?"
>
> Pilbeam: "We were."
>
> Leopoldo: "Very difficult to prove that logically, professor. Very difficult indeed."
>
> Sancho: "You mean that I may have received Communion?"
>
> Leopoldo: "You certainly did—in *his* mind. Does it matter to you?"
>
> Pilbeam: "There was no Host."
>
> Leopoldo: "Do you think it's more difficult to turn empty air into wine than wine into blood? Can our limited senses decide a thing like that? We are faced by an infinite mystery."
>
> Sancho: "I prefer to think there was no Host."
>
> Leopoldo: "Why?"
>
> Sancho: "Because once when I was young I partly believed in a God, and a little of that superstition still remains. I'm rather afraid of mystery, and I am too old to change my spots. I prefer Marx to mystery, father."

Pilbeam prefers facts to fiction, Sancho prefers Marx to mystery, and Fr. Leopoldo echoes the sentiments of St. Ambrose of Milan to the effect that if God can create *ex nihilo,* "out of nothing," all the more can he make of something that already exists something else.[393] And so the novel ends with Pilbeam taking Sancho to the nearest town, so that he can make his way to Portugal and escape the clutches of the Guardia Civil. There is no conversation between the two men, no Liturgy of the Word, but Sancho has his thoughts: "Why is it that the hate of a man—even of a man like Franco—dies with his death, and yet love, the love which he had begun to feel for Father Quixote, seemed now to live and grow in spite of the final separation and the final silence—for how long, he wondered with a kind of fear, was it possible for that love of his to continue? And to what end?"

Perhaps Sancho has discovered, in his own fashion, Señorita Martin's "Little Way of Love." Love changes everything, love is the logic of the universe, and love finds its final sacramental expression in the Eucharist. Mark Bosco, in his superb discussion of the novel, has this description of the Eucharist celebrated by Quixote and participated in by Sancho: "The spiritual force of their affection is textually consummated in a eucharistic rite that celebrates the exaltation of kenosis—self-emptying love—as the form of divine-human love. Now in the orbit of Quixote's love for him, Sancho moves into a state of doubt about what has just happened to him. . . . Though he tells [Fr. Leopoldo] that he still prefers Marxian certitude to mystery, the Mayor nonetheless wonders 'to what end' his love for the monsignor will lead him"[394]

(Endnotes)

1. Cross, *Early Christian Fathers*, 9.
2. Vokes, *Riddle*.
3. Ibid., 87.
4. See Niederwimmer, *Didache, A Commentary*, and Aaron Milavec, *The Didache: Faith, Hope and Life, 50–70 CE*.
5. O'Loughlin, *The Didache*.
6. Staniforth and Louth, "The Didache," 187.
7. For a clear and generally useful introduction to all of the major questions and challenges of *Didache* 9–10, one might consult Bradshaw, *Eucharistic Origins*, 24–42.
8. Betz, "Eucharist," 245.
9. Ibid., 249.
10. Ibid., 251.
11. O'Loughlin, *The Didache*, 94. It is interesting that Thomas O'Loughlin, in this excellent book on the *Didache*, mentions the regularity of meals with Jesus and others, but never adverts to the insightful work of LaVerdiere, SSS, *Dining*.
12. Staniforth and Louth, "The Didache," 194–97, with personal adaptations/translations from the Greek text.
13 . Couratin, "Liturgy," 139.
14. O'Loughlin, *The Didache*, 86.
15. Jasper and Cuming, *Prayers*, 20–21.
16. For the texts see Schmoller, *Handkonkordanz*, 377. For the meaning one might begin by consulting Bauer et al., *Greek-English Lexicon*, 609–10.
17. Of course, this is by no means certain. It has been pointed out, for example, that there are no clear parallels to the text in Ignatius of Antioch for in Theophilus of Antioch, and, indeed, that the earliest textual evidence for *The Didache* comes from Egypt. See Hawkins, "The Didache," 86. See also the useful remarks of Riggs, "Sacred Food," 274, and LaVerdiere, SS, *Eucharist*, 131.
18. Staniforth and Louth, "The Didache," 198, endnote 6.
19. Wainwright, *Eucharist and Eschatology*, 68.
20. Betz, "Eucharist," 272.
21. Jasper and Cuming, *Prayers*, 21.
22. Thus, Rordorf, "The Didache," 9.
23. Lietzmann, *Mass and the Lord's Supper*, 192–93.
24. Wainwright, *Eucharist and Eschatology*, 69.
25. A very good segue into the entire issue is provided by Bernier, SSS, *Ministry*,

chapters 1–3.

26. O'Loughlin, *The Didache*, 100–101.

27. Frend, *From Dogma to History*, cited in Thomas O'Loughlin, *The Didache*, 100.

28. Rordorf, "The Didache," 18.

29. Grant, *Greek Apologists*, 50.

30. Osborn, *Justin Martyr*, 201.

31. Norris, "The Apologists," 36.

32. Justin, *Apology*, 1.

33. He tells us about this in his *Dialogue with Trypho*, 2–8.

34. Chadwick, *Early Christian Thought*, 10.

35. Justin, *Dialogue with Trypho*, 8.

36. Lampe, *From Paul to Valentinus*, 259. Lampe writes: "A topographical identification is impossible. Nevertheless, the note indicates a rented apartment."

37. Barnard, *St. Justin Martyr*, 101.

38. See Buchanan, "Questions," 154.

39. LaVerdiere, SSS, *Eucharist*, 172.

40. Green, OSB, *Christianity*, 83.

41. Parvis, "Justin Martyr," 115–27.

42. Frend, *Rise of Christianity*, 175.

43. Radcliffe, OP, *What Is the Point?*, 16.

44. There is a useful and balanced discussion of this issue in Green, *Christianity*, 92–99.

45. See the discussion in Bradshaw, *Eucharistic Origins*, 64–68.

46. LaVerdiere, *Eucharist*, 173.

47. Following Jasper and Cuming, *Prayers*, 28–30.

48. Couratin, "Liturgy," 147, my emphasis.

49. Jourjon, "Justin," 75.

50. Ibid., 76.

51. Green, *Christianity*, 100.

52. Lampe, *From Paul to Valentinus*, 100.

53. Ibid., 101.

54. Jourjon, "Justin," 75.

55. Ibid.

56. See Cummings, *Deacons and the Church*.

57. Buchanan, "Questions," 152–55.

58. Hall, *Doctrine and Practice*, 81.

59. Cross, *Early Christian Fathers*, 155.

60. For the following see Cummings, *Eucharistic Doctors*, 26–29.

61. Hippolytus, cited in Greenslade, *Schism*, 48.

62. Ibid., 48–49.

63. Daniélou, Couratin, and Kent, *Historical Theology*, 73.

64. Dix, *Shape of the Liturgy*, 157.

65. Jones et al., *Study of Liturgy*, 87. A more detailed commentary on the difficulties and challenges posed by the text may be found in Bradshaw, *Reconstructing*, 47–52.

66. Stewart-Sykes, *Hippolytus*.

67. Old, *Reading and Preaching*, 274.

68. Cuming, "The Eucharist," 41.

69. Cuming, *Hippolytus*, 14.

70. I am following here the text as given in Jasper and Cuming, *Prayers*, 34–38.

71. Cuming, "The Eucharist," 43.

72. Ibid., 40.

73. Moloney, SJ, *Eucharistic Prayers*, 30.

74. See, for example, Danielou, SJ, *Christology*, 117ff, and Longenecker, *Christology*, 26.

75. Moloney, SJ, *Eucharistic Prayers*, 115, my emphasis.

76. Ibid., 33.

77. See, for example, Cuming, "The Eucharist," 45, and Bradshaw et al., *Apostolic Tradition*, 47–8.

78. Jasper and Cuming, *Prayers*, 33.

79. Dix and Chadwick, *Treatise*, 40.

80. Johnson, *Sacraments and Worship*, 286.

81. Dix, *Shape of the Liturgy*, 162.

82. Johnson, *Prayers*.

83. Ibid., 279.

84. Bouyer, *Eucharist*, 203.

85. Johnson, *Prayers*, 199, and especially his comments on page 233.

86. Rahner, SJ "Theology and the Arts," 24–25.

87. Hardy and Ford, *Praising and Knowing God*, 112.

88. Johnson, *Prayers*, 201.

89. Hardy and Ford, *Jubilate*, 155. For an autobiographical and final sense of Hardy's praise-centered theology see his very moving and posthumously published book, Daniel W. Hardy, *Wording a Radiance*.

90. Johnson, *Prayers*, 203.

91. Cooke, *Why Angels?*, 34.

92. Macquarrie, *Principles*, 234–37.

93. Bradshaw and Johnson, *Eucharistic Liturgies*, 39.

94. Jenkins, *Lost History*.

95. The text followed here is a conflation of that found in Jasper and Cuming, *Prayers*, 42–44, and Gelston, *Eucharistic Prayer*.

96. Burkitt, "Tatian's Diatessaron," 130.

97. See Soskice, *Sisters of Sinai*.

98. Hardy and Ford, *Praising and Knowing God*, 112.

99. The unpointed Syriac text is printed in Gelston, *Eucharistic Prayer*, 48–54.

100. Spinks, *Sanctus*, 206.

101. Fackre, "Angels Heard," 352.

102. See the discussion of Herbert in Cummings, *Eucharistic Doctors*, 196–202.

103. Driscoll, OSB, *Theology*, 165. This essay on the epiclesis is particularly fine.

104. Winkler, "New Witness," 117.

105. Taft, SJ, "Mass Without the Consecration?" 8.

106. Ibid., 8–9.

107. Ibid., 9.

108. Baldovin, SJ, *Bread of Life*, 114.

109. McKenna, C.M., *Eucharist and Holy Spirit*, 72.

110. Aquinas, ST 3a, q.78, a. 1, ad 4.

111. Cited in Cabié, *The Eucharist*, 147.

112. Cited in Taft, S.J., "The Epiclesis Question," 226.

113. Taft, "Mass without the Consecration?," 11

114. Macy, *Theologies*, 99.

115. Duffy, *Saints and Sinners*, 144–45.

116. Ibid., 145.

117. See Cummings, "Cardinal Robert Pullen and the Eucharist," *Emmanuel*, 615–19.

118. For details of Pullen's life and theology, see Courtney, SJ, *Cardinal Robert Pullen*.

119. Debate continues over Robert's teaching, whether it was in Exeter or Oxford, or in both places. In historical reference some confusion occurs because the Latin abbreviations for Exeter and Oxford are respectively *exon* and *oxon*. It is easy to see how a later scribe could have confused them, given the subsequent superiority of Oxford as a center of learning. Nonetheless, there remains a strong tradition for Robert's teaching at Oxford as well as Exeter. Here I follow Beryl Smalley over Reginald L. Poole. See Smalley, *Becket Conflict and Schools*, 39–40, Poole, "Early Lives," 61–70, especially 62–63.

120. See Letter 316 in Kienzle, *Letters*, 386–87.

121. Smalley, *Becket Conflict and Schools*, 40.

122. Courtney, *Cardinal Robert Pullen*, xi.

123. Ibid.

124. *Patrologia*, 186, 905–6, 919–22.

125. Smalley, *Beckett Conflict and Schools*, 42–43.

126. Courtney, *Cardinal Robert Pullen*, 220.

127. Goering, Oxford and Cambridge manuscripts, 158, cited in Cummings, "Cardinal Robert Pullen and Eucharist," 615.

128. This eucharistic tract has been appended by Goering to his article as Appendix B, 163–68, here 165.

129. *Patrologia*, 186, 961c. The verb is *vegetetur*, and the best contemporary expression for *vegere* seems to me to be "to vitalize."

130. Ibid., 963cd.

131. Ibid., 961d.

132. Ibid., 963c.

133. Poole, "Early Lives," 63.

134. Guy, *Thomas Becket*, 41.

135. Smalley, *Becket Conflict and Schools*, 109–11.

136. Ibid., 113.

137. Waddams, *St. Thomas Becket*, 6.

138. Guy, *Thomas Becket*, 314–35, provides a full account of the brutal murder based on all available evidence.

139. Smalley, *Becket Conflict and Schools*, 218.

140. Bell, "Baldwin of Ford," 234.

141. *The Oxford Dictionary of the Christian Church*, 123.

142. There is no English translation of the Latin treatise as far as I am aware. In this chapter I am reliant for the most part on the text in *Sources Chrétiennes*, 93, 94: *Baudouin de Ford, Le Sacrament de l'Autel*. Though there are two volumes, the pagination is sequential.

143. Bell, "Baldwin of Ford," 136.

144. Ibid., 142.

145. See Baldwin of Ford, *Le Sacrament de l'Autel*, 12.

146. Baldwin of Ford, *Le Sacrament de l'Autel*, 336–40.

147. Leclercq, *Love of Learning*, 82.

148. Leclercq, "Introduction," SA, 47.

149. Baldwin of Ford, *Le Sacrament de l'Autel*, 148.

150. Ibid., 204.

151. Ibid., 146–50.

152. Bell, "Baldwin of Ford," 149.

153. In Baldwin of Ford, *Le Sacrament de l'Autel*, 36.

154. Ibid., 364.

155. Leclercq, "Introduction," 39. See also Macy, *Theologies*, 194, fn. 216.

156. Smalley, *Becket Conflict*, 214.

157. Baldwin of Ford, *Le Sacrament de l'Autel*, 218–20.

158. Smalley, *Becket Conflict*, 219.

159. Thornton, *Margery Kempe*, 13.

160. Gallyon, *Margery Kempe of Lynn*, 14.

161. Windeatt, trans., *The Book of Margery Kempe*, ch. 1, 1. Hereafter, *The Book*.

162. While he was serving in Lynn, Sawtrey was examined before his bishop in 1399, and later, while serving in London, he was charged before the Archbishop of Canterbury, Thomas Arundel, with heresies, especially to do with transubstantiation.

163. See Atkinson, *Mystic and Pilgrim*, 103.

164. Windeatt, trans., *The Book*, ch. 8, 55.

165. Ibid., ch. 1, 42.

166. Ibid., ch. 3, 46.

167. thus, Atkinson, op. cit., 17.

168. Knowles, *English Mystical Tradition*, 146.

169. In Leclercq et al., *Spirituality*, 426.

170. Windeatt, trans., *The Book*, ch. 53, 168.

171. Ibid., ch. 17, 74.

172. Ibid., ch. 13, 63.

173. Thornton, *Margery Kempe*, 77.

174. A Benedictine of Stanbrook, "Margery Kempe and the Eucharist," 482. Col. Butler-Bowdon brought out his own translation of the book in 1936, and it is to this edition that the Benedictine refers. The manuscript once belonged to the library of the Carthusian monastery of Mount Grace, Yorkshire.

175. Windeatt, trans., *The Book*, ch. 5, 51.

176. Ibid., ch. 16, 72.

177. Gallyon, *Margery Kempe of Lynn*, 94.

178. Duffy, *Stripping*, 93.

179. Windeatt, trans., *The Book*, ch. 20, 83.

180. Ibid., ch. 48, 152–53. For more extended commentary see Duffy, *Stripping*, 109–10, and Rubin, *Corpus Christi*, 326–28.

181. For a clear presentation of Wyclif's views on spiritual authority that form the basis for some of his eucharistic opinions, see Macquarrie, *Stubborn Theological Questions*, 13–25. A thorough account of the eucharistic question among the Lollards is provided by Leff in his magisterial *Heresy*, 573–85.

182. For a thorough theological searching of the gift of tears, see Ross, *Fountain and Furnace*. Ross's analysis is very fine, though she gives little consideration to Western exemplars of tears, and Margery's copious weeping is never mentioned.

183. Windeatt, trans., *The Book*, ch. 32, 117.

184. Ibid., ch. 67, 202–203.

185. A Benedictine of Stanbrook, "Margery Kempe and the Eucharist," 473.
186. Duffy, *Stripping*, 19.
187. Windeatt, trans., *The Book*, ch. 82, 239.
188. Duffy, *Stripping*, 20.
189. Windeatt, trans., *The Book*, ch. 78, 227.
190. See Duffy, *Stripping*, 25.
191. Windeatt, trans., *The Book*, Book II, ch. 3, 274.
192. Ibid., ch. 72, 212.
193. Ibid., ch. 18, 78.
194. Ibid., ch. 28, 105.
195. Ibid., ch. 72, 212–13.
196. Atkinson, *Mystic and Pilgrim*, 13, emphasis added.
197. Ross, *Grief*, 122–25.
198. Gallyon, *Margery Kempe of Lynn*, 135.
199. Ibid., 27.
200. Windeatt, trans., *The Book*, 37, 127.
201. Gallyon, *Margery Kempe of Lynn*, 2.
202. Avis, "Hooker, Richard," 309.
203. Louis Bouyer, *Orthodox Spirituality*, 109.
204. McAdoo, "Richard Hooker," 107–109.
205. Cited in Moorman, *A History*, 217.
206. Nichols, OP, *Panther and Hind*, 40, slightly adapted.
207. Bouyer, *Orthodox Spirituality*, 109.
208. Walton, *Life of Mr. Richard Hooker*, 1644.
209. McAdoo, "Richard Hooker," 111.
210. Booty, *Reflections*, 3.
211. Lewis, *English Literature*, 459.
212. Hooker, *Ecclesiastical Polity*, 1.15.4.
213. Ibid., 5.7.1.
214. Ibid., 5.65.2.
215. Ibid., 5.8.2.
216. Ibid., 3.8.14.
217. McAdoo, "Richard Hooker," 118.
218. Booty, *Reflections*, 3.
219. Hooker, *Ecclesiastical Polity*, 5.56.10.
220. Ibid., 5.56.7.
221. Ibid., 5.57.1.
222. Ibid., 5.56.1.
223. Ibid., 2.11.2.
224. Williams, "Richard Hooker," 27.
225. Cocksworth, *Evangelical Eucharistic Thought*, 38.
226. Hooker, *Ecclesiastical Polity*, 5.67.1. For a complete account of Hooker's baptismal theology, see Stevenson, *Mystery*, 37–53.
227. Stevenson, *Covenant*, 34.
228. Hooker, *Ecclesiastical Polity*, 5.57.1.
229. Ibid., 5.67.2.
230. Ibid., 5.67.6.
231. Ibid., 5.67.11.

232. Booty, *Reflections,* 122.
233. Stevenson, *Covenant,* 29.
234. Hooker, *Ecclesiastical Polity,* 5.67.2.
235. Ibid., 5.67.3.
236. Ibid., 5.67.4.
237. Pattison, *Short Course,* 101.
238. Booty, *Reflections,* 4.
239. Greer, *Anglican Approaches,* xxvii.
240. Sevilla, SJ, Emeritus Bishop of Yakima, WA is something of an exception. Bishop Sevilla told me that while he was studying liturgy at the Institut Catholique in Paris, he wrote a paper on Lancelot Andrewes. This chapter is written in honor of Bishop Sevilla.
241. Wainwright, *Lesslie Newbigin,* 17.
242. Bouyer, Cong. Orat., *Orthodox Spirituality,* 117.
243. Higham, *Lancelot Andrewes,* 10.
244. Stevenson, "Andrewes, Lancelot," 74.
245. Cited in McAdoo, *Anglican Heritage,* 3.
246. Welsby, *Lancelot Andrewes, 1555–1626,* 44.
247. Ibid., 34.
248. Ibid., 12.
249. Wakefield, "Andrewes, Lancelot," 12.
250. See, for example, Caraman, *Henry Garnet,* and Fraser, *Faith and Treason,* especially 289–91.
251. Welsby, *Lancelot Andrewes,* 137.
252. Allchin, "Lancelot Andrewes," 145–46.
253. Stevenson, *Covenant,* 39.
254. Durning and Tilbury, "Looking unto Jesus," 490.
255. Ibid., 493.
256. Cited in Durning and Tilbury, "Looking unto Jesus," 509. I have altered the language somewhat to make the text flow more smoothly for the contemporary reader.
257. McCullough, "Lancelot Andrewes and Language," 305.
258. Chadwick, "Defence," 431.
259. Lossky, *Lancelot Andrewes.*
260. See Davis, *Imagination Shaped,* 9. Her treatment of Andrewes runs from pp. 9–62, and *Wondrous Depth,* 85–127.
261. Allchin, "Lancelot Andrewes," 151.
262. Ibid.
263. DeSilva, "Feast in the Text," especially 26.
264. Welsby, *Lancelot Andrewes,* 194–95.
265. Eliot, *For Lancelot Andrewes,* 24.
266. Cited from Stevenson, "Lancelot Andrewes on Ash Wednesday," 5.
267. Welsby, *Lancelot Andrewes,* 60.
268. Stevenson, "Lancelot Andrewes at Holyrood," 458.
269. Stevenson, "Andrewes, Lancelot," 74.
270. Dorman, *Lancelot Andrewes,* 99.
271. Allchin, "Lancelot Andrewes," 156.
272. Stevenson, *Mystery,* 64.
273. Lossky, *Lancelot Andrewes,* 208–88.
274. The sermon is cited in Stevenson, *Mystery,* 59.

275. Dorman, *Lancelot Andrewes*, 95.
276. Allchin, "Lancelot Andrewes," 157.
277. Ibid., 159.
278. Dorman, *Lancelot Andrewes*, 92.
279. Ibid.
280. Allchin, *Living Presence*, 61.
281. Stevenson, "Andrewes, Lancelot," 75.
282. Welsby, *Lancelot Andrewes*, 151.
283. This translation of Andrewes's Latin text comes from Stone, *A History*, 264ff.
284. According to his contemporaries, Buckeridge and Isaacson. See McAdoo, *Anglican Heritage*, 69.
285. Higham, *Lancelot Andrewes*, 108.
286. Ibid., 117.
287. Allchin, "Lancelot Andrewes," 150. See the comment of Ramsey, *Gospel and Catholic Church*, 206.
288. Allchin, "Lancelot Andrewes," 150.
289. Wakefield, "Andrewes, Lancelot," 11.
290. Brilioth, *Eucharistic Faith and Practice*, 215.
291. Battiscombe, *John Keble*, 11.
292. O'Connell, *Oxford Conspirators*, 91.
293. Ibid.
294. Bouyer, *Orthodox Spirituality*, 208.
295. Cited in Johnson, *John Keble*, 5.
296. Cited in Johnson, *Prayers*, 6.
297. Rowell, "John Keble," 244.
298. Chadwick, " Limitations," 47.
299. Dawson, *Spirit*, 12.
300. Rowell, "John Keble and the High Church Tradition," 22.
301. Rowell, "John Keble," 244.
302. Macquarrie, *Two Worlds Are Ours*, 218–22, slightly adapted.
303. Cited in Rowell, "John Keble," 246.
304. Keble, *Christian Year*, 42–43.
305. O'Connell, *Oxford Conspirators*, 93.
306. Macquarrie, *Two Worlds Are Ours*, 220.
307. Rowell, *Vision*, 24.
308. Johnson, *Prayers*, 10.
309. Ibid., 15.
310. Keble, *Letters*, 1870, 39, cited in Rowell, *Vision*, 37.
311. Johnson, *Prayers*, 29–31.
312. Rowell, *Vision*, 35.
313. Johnson, *Prayers*, 29.
314. Keble, *Christian Year*, 187.
315. Keble, *Sermons Academic and Occasional*, 260, 259, cited in Rowell, *Vision*, 36.
316. Cited in Rowell, "John Keble," 245.
317. Keble, "Primitive Tradition," 213, cited in Rowell, *Vision Glorious*, 34.
318. Chadwick, "Limitations," 50.
319. Keble, *On Eucharistical Adoration*, 75–76, cited in Rowell, *Vision*, 37.
320. Chadwick, *Mind of the Oxford Movement*, 30.

321. Towards the end of the poem "Gunpowder Treason."

322. Chadwick, *Mind of the Oxford Movement,* 31.

323. Griffin, *John Keble,* 71–74.

324. See Chadwick, "Limitations," 49.

325. Nicholl, *Holiness,* 28.

326. Rowell, *Vision,* 40.

327. Cited in Gilley, *Newman and His Age,* 339.

328. Dessain and Gornall, SJ, *Letters and Diaries,* 299.

329. Old, "Preaching as Worship," 113.

330. Long, *Eucharistic Theology,* Page references to the text will be provided in parentheses as we go along.

331. Ibid., 11.

332. Ibid., 15.

333. For Hildegard see Cummings, *Mystical Women,* 5–17.

334. Sermon 83, cited in Long, *Eucharistic Theology,* 22.

335. Ibid., 24–25.

336. Ibid., 30.

337. See Cummings, *Eucharistic Doctors,* 215–27.

338. Ibid., 40.

339. Gerrish, *Grace and Gratitude.*

340. Jasper, *Sacred Body,* 116.

341. Jasper and Cuming, *Prayers.*

342. See the brief but accurate appreciation of Geofrey Cuming provided by Gray, "Work of Geoffrey Cuming," 157–59.

343. Gray, *Ronald Jasper,* 6.

344. Ibid., 38.

345. Dix, OSB, *Shape of the Liturgy.*

346. George, "Ronald Jasper," 1.

347. Gray, *Ronald Jasper,* 94.

348. For a sense of Bradshaw's influence in liturgical studies as well as his own interests see. Johnson and Phillips, *Studia Liturgical Diversa.* For Spinks, see Ross and Jones, *Serious Business of Worship.*

349. Bugnini, *Reform of the Liturgy,* 199–202 (see also 415–17).

350. See Hardy and Ford, *Praising and Knowing God* for the importance of praise in worship and theology generally. More systematic reflections may be found in Ford and Stamps, *Essentials of Christian Community,* and Hardy, *God's Ways.*

351. Ibid., 140.

352. Jasper, "Eucharistic Body," 213.

353. Ibid., 215–16.

354. Ibid., 217.

355. Ibid., 218.

356. Ibid., 219.

357. Ibid., 221.

358. Crichton, "Theology of Worship," 28.

359. Crichton, "Bases for a Theology," 62.

360. Ibid., 63.

361. Ibid.

362. Ibid.

363. Crichton, "Worshipping," 452.

364. Grigassy, OFM, "J. D. Crichton's Significance."

365. Crichton, "Bases for a Theology," 63.

366. Ibid., 64.

367. Ibid., 63.

368. Ibid., 66.

369. Crichton, "Worshipping," 451.

370. Ibid., 453.

371. Ibid.

372. Nichols, OP, *Looking at the Liturgy.*

373. Crichton, Review of *Looking at the Liturgy,* 249–63.

374. Crichton, *Lights in the Darkness,* 10.

375. Crichton, Review of *Looking at the Liturgy,* 254–55.

376. Ibid., 256.

377. Bishop McMahon, "Dr. James Crichton," 4–5.

378. The text of the *laudatio* may be found in *Music and Liturgy* 21 (1995), 76–80.

379. Crichton, *Christian Celebration: The Mass,* 11.

380. Crichton, *Christian Celebration: The Prayer of the Church,* 11.

381. Crichton, Review of *Looking at the Liturgy,* 250.

382. Bosco, SJ, *Graham Greene's Catholic Imagination,* 152.

383. Cummings, "Grace," 68.

384. The edition I am using is Graham Greene, *Monsignor Quixote,* Introduction by John Auchard.

385. Auchard, "Introduction," xix.

386. Bosco, *Graham Green's Catholic Imagination,* 139. See, for detailed personal comment and insight, Duran, *Graham Greene.*

387. Bosco, *Graham Green's Catholic Imagination,* 140.

388. Ibid., 142.

389. Greene, *Monsignor Quixote,* 93.

390. Ibid., 66.

391. Bosco, *Graham Green's Catholic Imagination,* 152.

392. Ibid., 151.

393. See St. Ambrose of Milan, *On the Mysteries,* 52.

394. Bosco, *Graham Green's Catholic Imagination,* 149.

Bibliography

Allchin, A. M. "Lancelot Andrewes." In *The English Tradition and The Genius of Anglicanism*, edited by Geoffrey Rowell, 88–102. Nashville: Abingdon, 1992.

———. *The Living Presence of the Past*. New York: Seabury, 1981.

Atkinson, Clarissa W. *Mystic and Pilgrim: The Book and the World of Margery Kempe*. Ithaca, NY: Cornell University Press, 1983.

Avis, Paul. "Hooker, Richard." In *The Oxford Companion to Christian Thought*, edited by Adrian Hastings et al., 308–309. Oxford: Oxford University Press, 2000.

Baldovin, SJ, John F. *Bread of Life, Cup of Salvation*. Lanham, MD: Rowman and Littlefield, 2003.

Baldwin of Ford. *Sources Chrétiennes*, 93, 94: *Baudouin de Ford, Le Sacrament de l'Autel*. Introduction by Jean Leclercq, OSB; Latin edited by J. Morson, OCSO; French translation by E. de Solms, OSB. 2 vols. Paris: Cerf, 1963.

Barnard, Leslie. *St. Justin Martyr: The First and Second Apologies*. Ancient Christian Writers Series 56. Mahwah, NJ: Paulist, 1997.

Battiscombe, Georgina *John Keble: A Study in Limitations*. New York: Knopf, 1964.

Bauer, Arndt, et al., *A Greek-English Lexicon of the New Testament and Other Early Christian Literature*. Chicago: University of Chicago Press, 1957.

Bell, David N. "Baldwin of Ford and Twelfth Century Theology." In *Noble Piety and Reformed Monasticism*, edited by E. Rozanne Elder, 136–48. Kalamazoo, MI: Cistercian, 1981.

———. "Baldwin of Ford and the Sacrament of the Altar." In *Erudition at God's Service*, edited by John R. Sommerfeldt, 217–42. Kalamazoo, MI: Cistercian, 1987.

A Benedictine of Stanbrook. "Margery Kempe and the Eucharist." *The Downside Review* 56 (1938) 468–82.

Bernard, St. *The Letters of St. Bernard*, Translated by B. S. James, Introduction by B. M. Kienzle. Kalamazoo, MI: Cistercian, 1998.

Bernier, SSS, Paul. *Ministry in the Church, A Historical and Pastoral Approach*. New London, CT: Twenty-third, 1992.

Betz, Johannes. "The Eucharist in the Didache." In *The Didache in Modern Research*, edited by Jonathan A. Draper, 244–75. Leiden: Brill, 1996.

Booty, John. *Reflections on the Theology of Richard Hooker*. Sewanee, TN: The University of the South Press, 1998.

Bosco, SJ, Mark. *Graham Greene's Catholic Imagination*. Oxford: Oxford University Press, 2005.

Bouyer, Louis. *Eucharist*. Notre Dame, IN: University of Notre Dame Press, 1968.

Bibliography

————. *Orthodox Spirituality and Protestant and Anglican Spirituality.* New York: Desclée, 1969.

Bradshaw, Maxwell et al. *The Apostolic Tradition, A Commentary.* Minneapolis: Fortress, 2002.

Bradshaw, Paul F. *Eucharistic Origins.* Oxford: Oxford University Press, 2004.

————. *Reconstructing Early Christian Worship.* Collegeville, PA: Liturgical, 2009.

Bradshaw, Paul F., and Maxwell E Johnson. *The Eucharistic Liturgies.* Collegeville, PA: Liturgical, 2012.

Brilioth, Yngve. *Eucharistic Faith and Practice.* London: SPCK, 1969.

Buchanan, Colin. "Questions Liturgists Would Like to Ask Justin Martyr." In *Justin Martyr and his Worlds,* edited by Sara Parvis et al., 152–59. Minneapolis: Fortress, 2007.

Bugnini, Annibale. *The Reform of the Liturgy 1948–1975.* Collegeville, PA: Liturgical, 1990.

Burkitt, F. C. "Tatian's Diatessaron and the Dutch Harmonies." *Journal of Theological Studies* 25 (1924) 113–30.

Cabié, Robert. *The Eucharist.* Collegeville, PA: Liturgical, 1986.

Caraman, SJ, Philip. *Henry Garnet 1555–1606 and the Gunpowder Plot.* London: Longmans, Green and Co., 1964.

Chadwick, Henry. *Early Christian Thought and the Classical Tradition.* Oxford: Clarendon, 1966.

Chadwick, Owen. "A Defence of Lancelot Andrewes' Sermons." *Theology* 102 (1999) 431–35.

————. "The Limitations of Keble." *Theology* 67 (1964) 46–52.

————. *The Mind of the Oxford Movement.* Stanford, CA: Stanford University Press, 1960.

Cocksworth, Christopher. *Evangelical Eucharistic Thought in the Church of England.* Cambridge: Cambridge University Press, 1993.

Cooke, Bernard J. *Why Angels?* Mystic, CT: Twenty-third, 1996.

Couratin, Arthur H. "Liturgy." In *Historical Theology,* edited by Jean Daniélou et al., 139–240. Harmondsworth, UK: Penguin, 1969.

Courtney, SJ, Francis. *Cardinal Robert Pullen: An English Theologian of the Twelfth Century.* Rome: Gregorian University Press, 1954.

Crichton, James D. "The Bases for a Theology of the Liturgy." *The Ampleforth Journal* 84 (1979) 58–70.

————. *Christian Celebration: The Mass.* London: Chapman, 1971.

————. *Lights in the Darkness.* Dublin: Columba, 1976.

————. Review of *Looking at the Liturgy,* by Aidan Nichols, OP. *Liturgy* 20 (1996) 249–63.

————. "A Theology of Worship." In *The Study of Liturgy,* rev. ed., edited by Cheslyn Jones et al., 3–31. New York: Oxford University Press, 1992.

————. "Worshipping with Awe and Reverence." *Priests and People* 9 (1995) 475–52.

Cross, Frank D. *The Early Christian Fathers.* London: Duckworth, 1960.

Cuming, Geoffrey J. "The Eucharist." In *Essays on Hippolytus,* edited by Geoffrey J. Cuming, 39–51. Bramcote, UK: Grove, 1978.

————. *Hippolytus: A Text for Students.* Bramcote, UK: Grove, 1976.

Cummings, Owen F. "Cardinal Robert Pullen and the Eucharist." *Emmanuel* 107 (2001) 615–19.

————. *Deacons and the Church.* Mahwah, NJ: Paulist, 2004.

————. *Eucharistic Doctors.* Mahwah, NJ: Paulist, 2005.

————. *Mystical Women, Mystical Body.* Portland, OR: Pastoral, 2000.

————. *Thinking about Prayer.* Eugene, OR: Wipf and Stock, 2009.

Daniélou, SJ, Jean. *The Christology of Early Jewish Christianity.* Chicago: Regnery, 1964.

Davis, Ellen F. *Imagination Shaped: Old Testament Preaching in the Anglican Tradition.* Valley Forge, PA: Trinity, 1995.

———. *Wondrous Depth: Preaching the Old Testament.* Louisville, KY: Westminster-John Knox, 2005.

Dawson, Christopher. *The Spirit of the Oxford Movement.* Reprint. London: St. Austin, 2001.

DeSilva, David A. "'The Feast in the Text,' Lancelot Andrewes on the Task and the Art of Preaching." *Anglican Theological Review* 76 (1994) 9–26.

Dessain, C. S., and Thomas Gornall, SJ. *The Letters and Diaries of John Henry Newman.* Vol. 26. Oxford: Clarendon, 1974.

Dix, Gregory. *The Shape of the Liturgy.* London: Black, 1945.

Dix, Gregory, and Henry Chadwick. *The Treatise on the Apostolic Tradition of St. Hippolytus of Rome.* Ridgefield, CT: Morehouse, 1992.

Dorman, Marianne. *Lancelot Andrewes, A Perennial Preacher of the Post-Reformation English Church.* Tucson, AZ: Fenestra, 2004.

Driscoll, OSB, Jeremy. *Theology at the Eucharistic Table.* Rome: Centro Studi S. Anselmo, 2003.

Duffy, Eamon. *Saints and Sinners.* 2nd ed. New Haven: Yale University Press, 2001.

———. *The Stripping of the Altars.* New Haven: Yale University Press, 1992.

Duran, Leopoldo. *Graham Greene: An Intimate Portrait by His Closest Friend and Confidant.* London: HarperCollins, 1994.

Durning, Louise, and Clare Tilbury. "'Looking unto Jesus': Image and Belief in Seventeenth-Century English Chancel." In *Journal of Ecclesiastical History* 60 (2009) 490–513.

Eliot, T. S. *For Lancelot Andrewes: Essays on Style and Order.* Garden City, NY: Doubleday, Doran and Co., 1929.

Fackre, Gabriel. "Angels Heard and Demons Seen." *Theology Today* 51 (1994) 345–58.

Ford, David F., and Dennis L. Stamps. *Essentials of Christian Community.* Edinburgh: T. & T. Clark, 1996.

Fraser, Antonia. *Faith and Treason: The Story of the Gunpowder Plot.* Garden City, NY: Doubleday, 1996.

Frend, William H. C. *From Dogma to History: How Our Understanding of the Early Church Developed.* London: SCM, 2003.

———. *The Rise of Christianity.* Philadelphia: Fortress, 1984.

Gallyon, Margaret. *Margery Kempe of Lynn and Medieval England.* Norwich, UK: Canterbury, 1995.

Gelston, Andrew. *The Eucharistic Prayer of Addai and Mari.* Oxford: Clarendon, 1992.

George, Raymond. "Ronald Jasper: An Appreciation." In *Liturgy in Dialogue: Essays in Memory of Ronald Jasper,* edited by Paul Bradshaw et al., 1–8. Collegeville, PA: Liturgical, 1993.

Gerrish, Brian A. *Grace and Gratitude.* Minneapolis: Augsburg, 1993.

Gilley, Sheridan. *Newman and His Age.* London: Darton, Longman and Todd, 1990.

Grant, Robert M. *Greek Apologists of the Second Century.* Philadelphia: Westminster, 1988.

Gray, Donald. *Ronald Jasper: His Life, His Work and the ASB.* London: SPCK, 1997.

———. "The Work of Geoffrey Cuming: An Appreciation." In *Liturgy Reshaped,* edited by Kenneth Stevenson, 157–59. London: SPCK, 1982.

Green, OSB, Bernard. *Christianity in Ancient Rome, the First Three Centuries.* London: T. & T. Clark, 2010.

Bibliography

Greene, Graham. *Monsignor Quixote*. Introduction by John Auchard. London: Penguin, 2008.

Greenslade, S. L. *Schism in the Early Church*. London: SCM, 1953.

Greer, Rowan A. *Anglican Approaches to Scripture*. New York: Crossroad, 2006.

Griffin, John R. *John Keble, Saint of Anglicanism*. Macon, GA: Mercer University Press, 1987.

Grigassy, OFM, Daniel P. "J. D. Crichton's Significance for Pastoral Liturgy in England." PhD diss., Catholic University of America, 1985.

Guy, John. *Thomas Becket: Warrior, Priest, Rebel*. New York: Random House, 2012.

Hall, Stuart G. *Doctrine and Practice in the Early Church*. Grand Rapids, MI: Eerdmans, 1991.

Hardy, Daniel W., and David F. Ford. *Praising and Knowing God*. Philadelphia: Westminster, 1985.

Hardy, Daniel W. *God's Ways with the World*. Edinburgh: T. & T. Clark, 1996.

———. *Wording a Radiance: Parting Conversations on God and the Church*. London: SCM, 2010.

Hawkins, Frank. "The Didache." In *The Study of Liturgy*, rev. ed., edited by C. Jones, G. Wainwright, et al., 84–86. New York: Oxford University Press, 1992.

Higham, Florence. *Lancelot Andrewes*. London: SCM, 1952.

Jasper, David. "The Eucharistic Body in Art and Literature." In *Exchanges of Grace: Essays in Honour of Ann Loades*, edited by Natalie K. Watson et al., 213–23. London: SCM, 2008.

———. *The Sacred Body: Asceticism in Religion, Literature, Art, and Religion*. Waco, TX: Baylor University Press, 2009.

Jasper, Ronald C. D., and Geoffrey J. Cuming. *Prayers of the Eucharist, Early and Reformed*. 3rd ed. New York: Pueblo, 1987.

Jenkins, Philip. *The Lost History of Christianity*. New York: HarperCollins, 2008.

Johnson, Maria P. *John Keble: Sermons for the Christian Year*. Grand Rapids: Eerdmans, 2004.

Johnson, Maxwell E. *The Prayers of Sarapion: A Literary, Liturgical, and Theological Analysis*. Rome: Pontificio Istituto Orientale, 1995.

———. *Sacraments and Worship: The Sources of Christian Theology*. Louisville, KY: Westminster John Knox, 2012.

Johnson, Maxwell E., and Edward L. Phillips. *Studia Liturgica Diversa: Essays in Honor of Paul F. Bradshaw*. Portland, OR: Pastoral, 2003.

Jourjon, Maurice. "Justin." In *The Eucharist of the Early Christians*, edited by Willy Rordorf et al., 71–85. New York: Pueblo, 1978.

Keble, John. *The Christian Year*. London: Oxford University Press, 1914.

Knowles, OSB, David. *The English Mystical Tradition*. New York: Harper & Row, 1961.

Lampe, Peter. *From Paul to Valentinus: Christians at Rome in the First Two Centuries*. Minneapolis: Fortress, 2003.

LaVerdiere, Eugene SSS. *Dining in the Kingdom of God*. Chicago: Liturgy Training, 1994.

———. *The Eucharist in the New Testament and the Early Church*. Collegeville, PA: Liturgical, 1996.

Leclercq, Jean. *The Love of Learning and the Desire for God*. New York: Fordham University Press, 1982.

Leclercq, Vandenbroucke, et al. *The Spirituality of the Middle Ages*. London: Burns and Oates, 1968.

Leff, Gordon. *Heresy in the Later Middle Ages.* Manchester: Manchester University Press, 1999.

Lewis, C. S. *English Literature in the Sixteenth Century.* Oxford: Oxford University Press, 1954.

Lietzmann, Hans. *Mass and the Lord's Supper: A Study in the History of the Liturgy.* Leiden: Brill, 1979.

Long, Kimberly Bracken. *The Eucharistic Theology of the American Holy Fairs.* Louisville: Westminster John Knox, 2011.

Longenecker, Richard N. *The Christology of Early Jewish Christianity.* London SCM, 1970.

Lossky, Nicholas. *Lancelot Andrewes the Preacher (1555–1626).* Oxford: Clarendon, 1991.

McAdoo, Henry R. *Anglican Heritage: Theology and Spirituality.* Norwich, UK: Canterbury, 1991.

————. "Richard Hooker." In *The English Religious Tradition and the Genius of Anglicanism*, edited by Geoffrey Rowell, 78–87. Nashville: Abingdon, 1992.

McCullough, Peter E. "Lancelot Andrewes and Language." *Anglican Theological Review* 74 (1992) 304–16.

McKenna, C. M., John H. *Eucharist and Holy Spirit: The Eucharistic Epiclesis in Twentieth Century Theology.* Great Wakering, UK: Mayhew-McCrimmon, 1975.

McMahon, Thomas. "Dr. James Crichton." *Liturgy* 20 (1995) 4–5.

Macquarrie, John. *Principles of Christian Theology.* 2nd ed. New York: Scribner's Sons, 1977.

————. *Stubborn Theological Questions.* London: SCM, 2002.

————. *Two Worlds Are Ours: An Introduction to Christian Mysticism.* London: SCM, 2004.

Macy, Gary. *The Theologies of the Eucharist in the Early Scholastic Period.* Oxford: Clarendon, 1984.

Milavec, Aaron. *The Didache: Faith, Hope and Life of the Earliest Christian Communities, 50–70 CE.* Mahwah, NJ: Newman, 2003.

Moloney, SJ, Raymond. *The Eucharistic Prayers in Worship, Preaching and Study.* Wilmington, DE: Glazier, 1985.

Moorman, John R. H. *A History of the Church in England.* 3rd ed. London: Black, 1980.

Nicholl, Donald. *Holiness.* London: Darton, Longman and Todd, 1981.

Nichols, OP, Aidan. *Looking at the Liturgy.* San Francisco: Ignatius, 1996.

————. *The Panther and the Hind: A Theological History of Anglicanism.* Edinburgh: T. & T. Clark, 1993.

Niederwimmer, Kurt. *The Didache: A Commentary.* Minneapolis: Fortress, 1998.

Norris, Richard A. "The Apologists." In *Early Christian Literature*, edited by Frances M. Young et al., 36–44. Cambridge: Cambridge University Press, 2004.

O'Connell, Marvin R. *The Oxford Conspirators: A History of the Oxford Movement 1833–1845.* London: Collier-Macmillan, 1969.

Old, Hughes O. "Preaching as Worship in the Pulpit of John Calvin." In *Tributes to John Calvin*, edited by David W. Hall, 95–117. Phillipsburg, NJ: Presbyterian and Reformed, 2010.

————. *The Reading and the Preaching of the Scriptures in the Worship of the Christian Church.* Vol. 1. Grand Rapids: Eerdmans, 1998.

O'Loughlin, Thomas. *The Didache: A Window on the Earliest Christians.* London: SPCK, 2010.

Osborn, Eric F. *Justin Martyr.* Tübingen: Mohr, 1973.

Bibliography

Parvis, Sara. "Justin Martyr and the Apologetic Tradition." In *Justin Martyr and His Worlds,* edited by Sara Parvis et al., 115–27. Minneapolis: Fortress, 2007.

Pattison, George. *A Short Course in Christian Doctrine.* London: SCM, 2005.

Poole, Reginald L. "The Early Lives of Robert Pullen and Nicholas Breakspear." In *Essays in Early Medieval History Presented to Thomas Frederick Tout,* edited by A. G. Little et al., 61–70. Freeport, NY: Books for Libraries, 1967.

Radcliffe, OP, Timothy. *What Is the Point of Being a Christian?* New York: Continuum-Burns & Oates, 2005.

Rahner, SJ, Karl, "Theology and the Arts." *Thought* 57 (1982) 17–29.

Ramsey, Michael. *The Gospel and the Catholic Church.* 2nd ed. Cambridge, MA: Cowley, 1990.

Riggs, John W. "The Sacred Food of Didache 9-10." In *The Didache in Context,* edited by Clayton N. Jefford. Leiden: Brill, 1995.

Rordorf, Willy. "The Didache." In *The Eucharist of the Early Christians,* edited by Willy Rordorf et al., 1–23. New York: Pueblo, 1978.

Ross, Ellen M. *The Grief of God: Images of the Suffering Jesus in Late Medieval England.* Oxford: Oxford University Press, 1997.

Ross, Maggie. *The Fountain and the Furnace.* Mahwah, NJ: Paulist, 1987.

Ross, Melanie, and Simon Jones. *The Serious Business of Worship: Essays in Honour of Bryan D. Spinks.* London: T. & T. Clark, 2010.

Rowell, Geoffrey. "John Keble: A Bi-Centenary Sermon." In *The English Religious Tradition and the Genius of Anglicanism,* edited by Geoffrey Rowell, 198–204. Nashville: Abingdon, 1992.

———. "John Keble and the High Church Tradition." In his *The Vision Glorious,* 21–42. Oxford: Oxford University Press, 1983.

Rubin, Miri. *Corpus Christi: The Eucharist in Late Medieval Culture.* Cambridge: Cambridge University Press, 1991.

Schmoller, Alfred. *Handkonkordanz zum Griechischen Neuen Testament.* Stuttgart: Deutsche Bibelgesellschaft, 1982.

Smalley, Beryl. *The Becket Conflict and the Schools.* Totowa, NJ: Rowman and Littlefield, 1973.

Soskice, Janet. *The Sisters of Sinai: How Two Lady Adventurers Discovered the Hidden Gospels.* London: Vintage, 2010.

Spinks, Bryan D. *The Sanctus in the Eucharistic Prayer.* Cambridge: Cambridge University Press, 1991.

Staniforth, Maxwell, and Andrew Louth. "The Didache." In *Early Christian Writers,* 2nd ed., edited by Maxwell Staniforth and Andrew Louth, 185–99. London: Penguin, 1987.

Stevenson, Kenneth. "Andrewes, Lancelot," In *The SPCK Handbook of Anglican Theologians,* edited by Alister E. McGrath, 74–78. London: SPCK, 1998.

———. *Covenant of Grace Renewed: A Vision of the Eucharist in the Seventeenth Century.* London: Darton, Longman and Todd, 1994.

———. "Lancelot Andrewes at Holyrood: The 1617 Whitsun Sermon in Perspective." *Scottish Journal of Theology* 52 (1999) 455–75.

———. "Lancelot Andrewes on Ash Wednesday: A Seventeenth-Century Case Study on How to Start Lent." *Theology* 108 (2005) 3–13.

———. *The Mystery of Baptism in the Anglican Tradition.* Harrisburg, PA: Morehouse, 1998.

Stewart-Sykes, Alistair. *Hippolytus: On the Apostolic Tradition.* Crestwood, NY: St. Vladimir's Seminary Press, 2001.

Stone, Darwell. *A History of the Doctrine of the Holy Eucharist* II. London: Longmans, 1909.

Taft, S.J., Robert F. "The Epiclesis Question in the Light of the Orthodox and Catholic Lex Orandi Traditions." In *New Perspectives on Historical Theology, Essays in Memory of John Meyendorff,* edited by Bradley Nassif, 210–37. Grand Rapids: Eerdmans, 1996.

———. "Mass without the Consecration?" *America* 188 (2003) 7–11.

Thornton, Martin. *Margery Kempe: An Example in the English Pastoral Tradition.* London: SPCK, 1960.

Vokes, Frederick E. *The Riddle of the Didache.* London: SPCK, 1938.

Waddams, Herbert. *St. Thomas Becket.* London: Pitkin, 1969.

Wainwright, Geoffrey. *Eucharist and Eschatology.* 2nd ed. London: Epworth, 1978.

———. *Lesslie Newbigin: A Theological Life.* Oxford: Oxford University Press, 2000.

Wakefield, Gordon S. "Andrewes, Lancelot." In *A Dictionary of Christian Spirituality,* edited by Gordon S. Wakefield, 11–12. London: SCM, 1983.

Welsby, Paul A. *Lancelot Andrewes, 1555–1626.* London: SPCK, 1964.

Williams, Rowan D. "Richard Hooker: Contemplative Pragmatism." In *Anglican Identities,* 40–56. Cambridge, MA: Cowley, 2003.

Windeatt, B. A., translator. *The Book of Margery Kempe.* Harmondsworth, UK: Penguin, 1994.

Winkler, Gabriele. "A New Witness to the Missing Institution Narrative." In *Studia Liturgica Diversa: Essays in Honor of Paul F. Bradshaw,* edited by Maxwell E. Johnson et al., 117–28. Portland, OR: Pastoral, 2004.

Lightning Source UK Ltd.
Milton Keynes UK
UKOW05f2154030214

225820UK00017B/1089/P